I0565896

Loyal to the Game

Lock Down Publications & Ca$h Presents
Loyal to the Game

.

Lock Down Publications

P.O. Box 1482
Pine Lake, Ga 30072-1482

Visit our website at
www.lockdownpublications.com

Copyright 2017 Loyal to the Game

All rights reserved. No part of this book may be reproduced in any form or by electronic or mechanical means, including information storage and retrieval systems without permission in writing from the publisher, except by a reviewer who may quote brief passages in review.

First Edition July 2017
Printed in the United States of America
This is a work of fiction. Names, characters, places, and incidents either are products of the author's imagination or are used fictitiously. Any similarity to actual events or locales or persons, living or dead, is entirely coincidental.

Cover design and layout by: Dynasty's Cover Me
Book interior design by: Shawn Walker
Edited by: Lauren Burton

Stay Connected with Us!

Text **LOCKDOWN** to 22828 to stay up-to-date
with new releases, sneak peaks, contests and more…

Thank you!

Submission Guideline.

Submit the first three chapters of your completed manuscript to ldpsubmissions@gmail.com, subject line: Your book's title. The manuscript must be in a .doc file and sent as an attachment. Document should be in Times New Roman, double spaced and in size 12 font. Also, provide your synopsis and full contact information. If sending multiple submissions, they must each be in a separate email.

Have a story but no way to send it electronically? You can still submit to LDP/Ca$h Presents. Send in the first three chapters, written or typed, of your completed manuscript to:

LDP: Submissions Dept
Po Box 1482
Pine Lake, Ga 30072

DO NOT send original manuscript. Must be a duplicate.

Provide your synopsis and a cover letter containing your full contact information.

Thanks for considering LDP and Ca$h Presents.

T.J. & Jelissa

Prologue

Then it happened, the same night they had chosen to stay in. They were in the bedroom, in the midst of making sweet, passionate love, the kind that's rough and intimate, getting fully in tune with each other's senses, when their bedroom door was kicked open. Ten masked men in all black surrounded the bed and smacked Avery on the back of the head with the handle of a gun, knocking him out. He fell on top of her and was dragged from her body. Then she was snatched up and forced into a chair. They tied her arms behind her and her legs to each other. She felt a blow to the back of her head, and everything faded to black.

***

When she came to, a caramel-skinned man in a bulletproof vest was holding something under her nose that smacked her senses and made her want to run. She tried to move, but couldn't. Her hands and legs were bound. The corner of her mouth felt sore. She looked to her right and saw Avery sitting next to her, also bound and gagged. The both of them were naked as jaybirds.

The caramel-skinned man walked over to Avery and held the same thing under his nose that had jarred her awake. Avery slowly came to. When he regained his senses, he tore his head away from the man's hand.

Tiny didn't know where they were, but they were no longer at her condo. They were in some kind of a basement – a grungy basement. She'd seen more than four rats skitter across the floor already. She became scared and wondered what the men wanted with them.

The caramel-skinned man was the only one without a mask. Inside the room were at least 15 other people, masked and heavily armed. All Tiny could see were the pupils of their eyes.

The caramel-skinned man walked over to Avery, took the gag out of his mouth and knelt down.

Avery smacked his lips together before finding his voice. "What the fuck is going on, Chris? Why am I and my lady down here?" he asked through a dry, raspy voice.

Chris laughed. "Well, ain't it obvious?" He stood up and ran his hand through the air. "You already know what it means when you show up down here on the receiving end. It means you done fucked up, nigga! So tell me, Avery, what have you did to fuck up?"

Avery struggled against his bonds. "Man, I ain't did shit, and you know it. You just fucking with me because you can. I ain't never did nothing to you, Chris, but try to have your back. I don't get why you doing this shit."

Chris took a cigar out of the inner pocket of his suit jacket and lit it. He blew the smoke straight into the air. "Wow, those are some strong words there, brother. You sure you don't want to take none of that back? I mean, at least for your woman's sake over here?" Chris walked over to Tiny and put his hand on her shoulder. He reached down and snatched the gag out of her mouth. "What's your name, little sister?"

She smacked her lips together and tried to swallow her spit because her mouth was so dry. "My name is Tiny, and I haven't done anything to you, so why am I here?"

Chris inhaled the smoke into his lungs and blew it into her face. "Avery, I have to admit, this little lady right here is fine as a muthafucka. I don't know where you found her at, but lucky you. It's a shame we gon' have to take her off this earth."

Tiny started crying as soon as she heard those words. She knew the man was serious. She saw her life flash before her eyes. She thought about her mother, her father, Ariana, and her favorite Aunty Gwen whom she had not visited in a while. She missed her so much, and she promised herself if she made it out of this debacle, she would drive over to her home in Riverdale just to hug and kiss her.

"Chris, why are you doing this? What have I done to deserve this treatment?"

Chris spun on the balls of his feet and stopped directly in front of Avery. "You brought that thieving-ass nigga Red into the fold, and he done made off with 75 thousand dollars, and now he can't be found! So, you tell me where he is, and where the money is, and I'll spare your lives. That don't mean I'm not fucking you up, though. You gon' feel this steel, that's law! But I will let you live."

Tiny closed her eyes. She knew they were dead meat. There was no way Avery knew where Red was. If he had known, he would have told her, and he would have been prepared to face their impending onslaught. She could tell he was completely caught off guard, and that worried her.

"Chris, you know I would never cross King, man. That's my blood. I don't know what's going on with Red, but whatever he did, I ain't have no knowledge of it. I have cleaned up after him before. I can't keep doing that shit, bro. I got my own life to think about."

Chris walked up to him and stubbed the blunt out on his neck. Avery screamed at the top of his lungs and Tiny started crying. She could smell the mixture of weed and skin floating through the air.

"Nigga, all I'm hearing you say is you don't know where our money is, which means you have to be chastised. That's $75,000. That's a whole lot of money. I have to go in front of King and explain how I fucked up by putting y'all into position to handle that load. Do you understand me?" *Chris lit the blunt again and blew the smoke toward the ceiling.* "So, tell me, Avery, what am I supposed to do about this loss? And be careful, because the next time I put out this blunt it's gon' be on your li'l girlfriend over here."

The hole in his neck still had smoke coming from it. "Chris, I don't know what you want me to say. I don't get down like that. I would never cross y'all. I got about 15 thousand put up of my own money, and I can do what I gotta do to get the rest, but I swear to you I'm innocent."

Chris grabbed Tiny by the hair, pulled her head backward, and stubbed the blunt out in the same spot he had put it out on Avery's neck. She screamed at the top of her lungs. The pain was so excruciating she shot up from the seat and wound up falling onto her side on the floor.

Chris laughed. "Well, damn, one thing we know for sure is baby girl ain't no masochist."

Avery tried to break his bonds. "Come on, Chris, man, that shit ain't funny. She didn't do nothing to you, and she ain't got nothing to do with this. You know King don't be condoning us hurting women. You're real foul right now, bro, for real."

Chris walked up to him and backhanded him across the face. "Nigga, fuck what you talking about, and fuck that bitch! King don't condone niggaz stealing from his organization, either. Now, you tell me what you gon' do about this money, or I'm about to leave both of y'all stanking and then throw you in that incinerator over there."

Tiny struggled to sit up, the pain in her neck unbearable. "I can get the money."

Chris stepped over to her form. "What did you just say?"

She flinched, thinking he was about to strike her. "Please, Chris, I can get the money. Just don't hurt us anymore, please."

Chris squinted his eyes. "Damn, my bad, shorty." He reached down and pulled her up and back into the seat. "Now, how are you going to get this money?"

"Look, I'll need a couple of days, but no more than three, and I promise you I'll have the remaining 60 thousand. We can add that to his 15 thousand, and that will give you 75 on the head. Will that be cool?"

Chris turned to look at Avery. "Wait a minute,

that 15 thousand is already cashed in. Avery, you gon' pay that just for taking us through all of this. So, it's either your girl gon' have to come up with the whole 75, or I'm gon' have to kill you, bro. And trust me, it will be my pleasure."

Tiny spoke up. "Wait a minute, you can't kill him."

Chris turned and gave her a look as if she'd just insulted him. "And why the fuck not?"

"Because I'm pregnant with his baby."

Chapter 1
1990
Before Me

Tiny plopped down on the couch and tore the heels off of her feet. She let out a loud groan before reaching down, grabbing her right foot, and slowly rubbing the bottom. Her ankle popped from the angle she had to bend her foot in order to get to the problem area. She had been diagnosed with plantar fasciitis at the tender age of 15. Now 16 and being forced to walk up and down the avenue all in the name of work, this only caused her condition to become worse.

Jaheim strolled into the living room, looked down on her, and then rolled his eyes. He was so used to her being a Drama Queen, it was starting to get old and a little tired.

He reached into his pocket and pulled out a little packet. He tore it open over the mirror he had just placed on his lap. The white, powdery substance spilled out, and he immediately began chopping through it with his razor blade.

Tiny groaned again, this time a little louder, trying to get his attention. He continued to snort the powder up his nose, completely ignoring her, and this irritated her to an unexplainable point.

She groaned again, this time so loud it was obvious. And again, he paid her no attention.

"Gotdamn, Jaheim, you hear me over here trying to get your attention. I don't know why you're purposely ignoring me!" she said, sticking a finger into her ear and shaking it, trying to get the itching within to stop.

He smiled and shook his head. "Girl, what's the matter with you now? Every time we come from working you always act like something wrong with your ass. I ain't got time for that shit tonight. You gon' rest them feet a little bit, then you gon' get your ass right back out there. We got a whole lot more hustling to do." He bent his head back down and tooted a hard line of cocaine, then coughed, growling in his throat as he felt the numbing sensation take him over.

"We? We? There you go with this *we* shit again. Nigga, *we* ain't doing shit. I'm the one that's out there lying on my back for these nasty-ass men. You ain't doing shit but sticking your hand out and waiting for me to hand you the money I busted my ass for, just so you can snort that shit up your nose. So you can stop hollering this *we* shit, 'cause it's really just some *me* shit!" She rolled her eyes and began rummaging through her purse for the already-rolled Phillys Blunt.

Jaheim lit a cigarette and blew the smoke to the ceiling. "Bitch, don't start that punk shit right now. I ain't trying to hear that dumb shit you getting ready to kick. Every time you bring yo' ass off them streets, you get to kicking the same shit! Shut yo' muthafucking mouth and smoke that li'l blunt. We gon' let them feet rest a little bit more, get you something to eat, then you gon' take your ass back out there and get *our* money." He tooted up another line hard, ran his tongue across his lips, and then frowned as he saw a huge rat crawl from under the refrigerator. It began slowly to move across the kitchen, stopping every few paces to sniff the area around it. Jaheim narrowed his eyes when he saw two smaller baby rodents crawl from under the same refrigerator and follow the path their mother was taking.

"Nigga, you always making it seem like you checking me. Let's get one thing straight: you definitely ain't checking this bitch right here. The only reason I get out there and do what I do is because I love yo' stupid ass. It ain't because I fear you or I'm scared of you, and definitely ain't because you checking me. I know this is our only hustle, and if we gon' be able to eat, then I'm gon' have to go out there and do my thang. Obviously this is all you know, so we can't depend on you to provide for us. But that's my fault for not following my dreams and choosing to follow yo ass all around Chicago like you some type of god or something. I've made my bed, so it's cool."

She put the flame to the end of the thickly-rolled cigar, then began to pull from it until the heavy smoke invaded her lungs, making her cough and blow out harshly. The smoke went down the wrong pipe, causing her to stand up and began beating on her chest, coughing over and over again, feeling the rawness in her throat. She felt like she was choking.

She dropped the blunt in the ashtray and ran into the kitchen with the intention of grabbing a juice from the refrigerator, but as soon as she got there she saw all three of the rodents and spun around so fast her foot got caught on the back of the other one, causing her to trip herself and fall flat on her back. She began screaming at the top of her lungs out of sheer terror.

All three rats shot past her, the mother jumping over her body and the two babies crawling over her, screeching to their escape. They ran out of the kitchen and down the short hallway toward the two bedrooms and disappeared.

Meanwhile, Jaheim was lying on his back on the couch laughing so hard he passed gas twice, there were tears running down his cheeks, and his stomach hurt so bad he silently prayed he could stop laughing, but he couldn't. He was laughing so hard he started to take his shirt off because he was starting to get hot.

"I don't see shit funny!" Tiny screamed, shooting up from the floor and dusting herself off. She felt like she was itching all over, and like one of the animals had somehow crawled up her pants leg. She started to scratch herself and jerked her shoulders in a fashion that said she was freaking out. "You lying yo' ass over there laughing, let's see how funny shit get when I take my ass in there and go to sleep. Fuck them streets. I ain't going back out there, and that's that!"

She started to peek down the hallway, trying to locate the creatures. She was so sick of living in the projects. She always swore to herself when she was a little girl that when she was old enough, she would flee the diseased habitat. She swore she would never allow the buildings to trap her, and she would find her way out. Being in love with Jaheim was somehow managing to counteract that. She prayed every single night that the love she had for him would fade and she would begin to love herself more than him. She wondered how she had allowed herself to turn against her family for a man that wanted nothing out of life. She knew she had broken her mother's heart because ever since then she and her mother had been at odds with one another. They could not be in the same room without an argument starting. All it took was the wrong look, and before you knew it they were in the middle of the street, seemingly fighting to the death, though it never went that far.

Jaheim jumped up off of the couch and ran over until he was standing in her face. He then leaned down and bumped his forehead into her smaller one. She could smell his stale breath as it radiated through his nostrils. The hot skin of his forehead was peppered with sweat, causing their heads to mold into one another's.

"Tiny, I swear to God, you better quit playing with me. Now, we leaving here in a half an hour. You take your ass back out there and get us this money, and that's gon' be that. You also gon' quit running your mouth so much to me like I'm one of them soft-ass niggas out there we be selling your pussy to. You starting to take my kindness for weakness. Don't have me beat your ass all up and down these projects. Don't think that shit can't happen."

He pressed his head harder into hers. He stood 5 feet, 10 inches tall, and his body was ripped from doing so many short jail bids. His dark black skin and brown eyes gave him the illusion of a handsome saint, but she knew underneath it all he was a goon. She noted the way his chest was rising and falling and knew he was riled up and meant business.

"Did you hear what the fuck I said, bitch?"

Now Tiny's blood began to get red hot. She hated when a man called her a bitch. It made her feel less than human. She grew up hearing that slur from her mother again and again, and it got even worst when her father thought calling her that was the cutest thing in the world.

Before she could think about what she was doing and what consequences it would have on her, she took a step backward, then fully extended both hands and pushed Jaheim forcibly out of her face. "Nigga, you better watch your mouth. I ain't no bitch! And I ain't gon' do shit I don't want to do. You don't scare me. My daddy been whopping my ass my whole life, so I'm prepared for whatever you think you gon' try to do. But I'm telling you now that shit ain't gon' be easy. We about to fight in this muthafucka!"

Jaheim stumbled back a few paces, then caught his balance. He looked down at the floor, then back over to the 5-foot, 1-inch light-skinned girl who couldn't possibly weigh more than 120 pounds. She balled up her little fists and scrunched up her pretty face, then yelled for him to come on and do what he gotta do.

He took a deep breath. "Tiny, stop playing with me. You know I ain't gon' put my hand on you unless you make me. But you taking your ass out there, and you gon' stay until we reach that quota. That's how it's about to work, point blank, period. So quit playing and take your ass in there and wash up."

Tiny snarled, "Nigga, fuck you! Like I said, I ain't going back out there, and that's point blank, period, or whatever the fuck you just said. You don't own me. Matter fact, I'm done. Period. I ain't selling my body no more for your lame ass. What the fuck was I thinking? You better get your li'l black ass out there and sell your dick for a change. Let me sit back and do nothing, then I'll take whatever you make and spend it all on weed, just like you spend all mine on cocaine." She shook her head. "What the fuck was I thinking? I had to be crazy." She turned to walk away.

As soon as she did, Jaheim was on her heels. He grabbed a hand full of her hair and yanked it so hard that her neck snapped backward. He then slammed her to the ground, and straddled her.

"Bitch, you think it's a game? You think I won't whoop your ass?" He slapped her across the face, then placed his hands around her neck and began to squeeze.

Tiny gagged. "Jaheim, let me up. I can't breathe." She tried kicking her legs and thrusting her pelvis upward, but nothing got him off of her.

"Aw, now you copping pleas. Now you sound all submissive and shit. What happened to that gangsta shit you was just kicking a few seconds ago? Mighty crazy how a bitch just transform from one character to the next. You gotta be bipolar, huh?" He squeezed her neck tighter smiling at the way her eyes began to roll toward the back of her head. Her body began to go limp, so he loosened his grip and stared down at her form.

She struggled to regain consciousness. As soon as she was strong enough to talk, she said, "Okay, daddy. I'm going to be a good girl now, but can you fuck the shit out of me for disobeying you? Please, daddy, because I need it."

Chapter 2

"But don't that seem weird to you, though, that you gon' be selling pussy for your brother? I mean, ain't that crossing some type of social line?" Tiny asked the dark, skinny girl who had just turned 18 years old.

Brandy paced back and forth in front of Tiny, smiling, before she stopped and shrugged her shoulders. She knew she had the body of a goddess, and growing up the only thing she ever aspired to be was a stripper and a female who made money off of men. Being raised in the projects hadn't allowed her to dream about things she could not imagine. She had never met anyone successful or famous, so those things just didn't exist in her mind. They were fictitious. Her reality was she had an amazing body. She saw the way men gawked at her, and she knew they would pay to play. She was tired of starving and going without. She knew the token to her survival was right between her legs.

At least that's what Jaheim had been telling her ever since she was 14 years old and busting out of the seams in her clothes. She could not wait until she turned 18. Today was her 18th birthday, and the only gift she wanted was for her brother to take her under his wing and put her on the track. A track that would run straight to green presidents.

"Girl, that shit don't bother me. So what if he my brother? At least I know he genuinely care about me, and he won't let nothing bad happen to me. If I wind up fucking with some other pimp, that nigga could wind up killing me one day. At least I know my brother got my back, and he has my best interest at heart," she said, sitting down on the couch and squirting baby oil into the palm of her hand then slapping it on to one thick chocolate thigh and rubbing it in. She repeated the process and did the same thing with the other thigh, then stood up in her shorts that were so small they were basically pointless.

Tiny shrugged her shoulders, "I mean I guess you're right if you're looking at it like that." She took another toke from her weed-filled cigar. "But you do know sometimes he be in the room while I'm servicing a trick, and some tricks even want him in the room to watch them ravish me? Shit, some tracks pay me more to let Jaheim fuck me in front of them. What happens if something like that comes up."

Brandy shrugged her shoulders. "Girl, I don't care. It's all about making money. If at the end of the day that's what it takes, and whoever the trick is putting out that bread, then I'm all for it. Whatever Jaheim want me to do, I'm gon' do it, because I ain't about to have him whooping my ass like he be doing you. I think it'll be so much easier to just listen." She reached over to grab the blunt from Tiny.

Tiny gave it to her, still perplexed by what the girl had said she was willing to do with Jaheim just to make some money. She shook her head. She didn't think it was that much money making in the world. She loved him, there was no doubt about that, but she wasn't sure she would be willing to cross that type of line in order to please him.

Jaheim came into the small living room and sat on the couch beside his little sister and kissed her on the cheek. "Happy birthday, baby girl. You're finally old enough to go out there and help me get this money. Are you sure you're ready?" he asked, kissing her on the cheek again and taking the blunt from her.

She nodded. "I'm ready to do whatever you need me to do. I'm following your lead. I just want to make you happy."

He wrapped his arm around her neck. "That's what I'm talking about. Let's do it, then."

As he finished those words, there was a knock at the door. He got up and asked who it was. At hearing the right words, he took the chain off the door and moved to the side as two older men stepped into the apartment, shaking his hand and giving him a half-hug.

Tiny noted the two men only lived a few doors down. They had lived in the Stateway Projects ever since she was a little girl. They had often given her quarters as a kid so she would be able to buy ice cream on those hot days. She knew they were brothers, and both men stayed with their ailing mother.

She had no idea what they were doing in her living room, because they were also deacons at her family's church. It didn't take long for her to figure that out, though, because both men were staring down at Brandy with lust in their eyes. They were actually salivating at the mouth.

"Damn, Brandy, you sho' done got fine over the years. Seem like just yesterday you was running up and down these hallways with pigtails in your hair. Now look at you, looking like a black stallion. I got to get me some of that," Derrick, the older brother, said while reaching into his pocket and handing Jaheim a $50 bill.

"Me, too." Lincoln followed and also gave Jaheim a $50 bill.

"Wait a minute. I told y'all $100. I wasn't saying $100 total, I was saying $100 apiece. Somebody ain't gon' be fucking, because all I got is a hundred dollars in my hand when I should have two, and there ain't no refunds. So, who gon' sit this one out?" he asked, looking from one man to the next.

"What, man?" Lincoln whined. "Aw, come on, Jaheim, you should have made that perfectly clear. I ain't never spent no $100 on no pussy before, man. I can do down on Federal Street and pick up 10 hos for $100, and you telling me all I get is this one? Nigga, you got to be out of your mind!"

"Yeah, man. What make her so special that we should be paying her 10 times the next ho?" said the brother.

"Nigga, you know damn well if you paying a bitch $10 for some pussy, she ain't nothing but a dope addict, and nine times out of 10 her pussy ain't no good. It's wore out, it's old, and it got more miles on it than I-94. This here is prime. It's fresh. Grade-A. Stand up, baby, and let them get a look at you."

Brandy stood up and allowed Jaheim to twirl her around in a circle. She ended with her back to the men. Jaheim reached around and cuffed her ass cheeks, which were already peeking out of her short shorts.

"You see what I'm saying? Look at how this ass bounce back every time I let it go." He gripped it again and again to emphasize his point. And sure enough, it bounced every time he let it go.

Both men looked at each other, then they went into their pockets and came out with another $50 apiece and handed it to Jaheim.

Jaheim smiled and whispered into Brandy's ear to make him proud. She disappeared down the hallway with an arm draped around each man's neck.

As soon as he heard the door close, Jaheim pumped a fist into the air and began grinning like the Cheshire Cat. "That girl gon' make me rich. I'm glad her little ass is as fine as she is, and it's a plus she love sex."

Tiny grunted, "Oh, yeah? How you know that?"

Jaheim was already putting the $200 around the knot he had in his pocket. "I know because that's my sister. All the women in our family are hot-blooded. It is what it is. That's also the reason all the men in my family are pimps. Yin and yang, baby. It's a balance – a balance that's gon' make me a lot of money.

Brandy could be heard in the background, moaning at the top of her lungs. This made Jaheim smile even harder.

"I bumped this li'l white bitch today, too. I guess she running away from her parents. I'm waiting for her to get all her stuff from her aunt's house, then I'm gon' put her ass down with us. I'm trying to build us an empire. All you gotta do is play yo' role. You gon' always be my bottom bitch," he said, wrapping his arm around her neck and kissing her on the cheek. "Tiny, I want you to look out for my little sister, though, and make sure she straight out there when I ain't in sight. We have to protect that investment."

Tiny shrugged up from under him. "Is that all she is to you, some kind of an investment?"

"Damn, don't start this dumbass shit. You know what the fuck I mean!"

"Nigga, no, I don't. And I'm starting to figure it out, though, because if that's how you think about your sister, I can only imagine what you really think and feel about me. So tell me, Jaheim, what it really is? What's going on with us? What am I to you?"

He rolled his eyes. "Every fucking day it's something new with you. You always got to find a way to bring some drama, huh? Well, I'm in a good mood. I got two new hos, and I'm about to get this money, and you ain't about to kill my vibe. If you don't know what you are to me, then I guess that mean we ain't clicking like we used to be. Shit, oh well." He shrugged his shoulders and pulled a pop out of the refrigerator.

"Oh well? Nigga, did you just say 'oh well?' What the fuck do that mean?" she asked, walking up on him and pulling on his shoulder until he turned around to face her, in the process spilling grape pop on to his white t-shirt.

"Fuck! What is your problem? Bitch, you got me spilling shit all on myself. Get the fuck out of my face before I whoop your ass for real."

"Fuck you, Jaheim. I wanna know what I am to you. Now that you snatching up all these other hos when I been with your dirty ass since the beginning, you coming at me like I'm just some bitch you pimping. You gotta come more correct than that. So, who am I?" she asked, pulling on his shirt and ripping it.

He swatted her hand away in one motion, and in the second motion he smacked her so hard she wound up doing a complete 180 before falling against the stove. He grabbed her by the back of the head and threw her into the garbage can, causing trash to spill everywhere and what seemed like a million roaches to scatter for cover.

"Bitch, I told you about playing with me. I told you about gettin' all up in my face and shit. Now I'm about to whoop your ass like I should have done a long time ago. Get yo punk-ass up!" Tiny struggled to get up. She felt woozy, and she was seeing two of him. She tasted blood in her mouth, and it felt like she had cracked a rib when he threw her into the garbage can. She felt the roaches crawling between her fingers as she struggled to get onto her feet.

Before she had the chance, he was grabbing her by the blouse and smacking her again. She landed right back in the trash.

"You just gotta make me whoop your ass. You act like you're addicted to this shit. I hate putting my hands on you, but if that's the only way you gon' respect this pimping, then I ain't got no muthafucking choice." He pulled his belt from his pants and gripped the buckle in his hands, then proceeded to slash her again and again, causing large welts to appear across her back and arms, and even her face.

She started to scream. "Jaheim, please! You're hurting me! Oh my god!" she cried. But her screams and tears were to no avail.

He continued to beat her again and again until he felt his arm giving out, then he knelt down on the floor and began ripping her clothes off. Once nude, he trapped himself between her legs, entered her body, and took her like a vicious thug for the next hour.

Chapter 3

"Daddy, I gotta admit that you do treat me so good, though. I'm glad I'm selling this pussy for you and not one of these other lame-ass, unworthy niggas," Brandy said, and she stood on tiptoe and kissed Jaheim on the cheek.

Tiny stayed silent under his other arm as they walked through the shopping mall. They had been working constantly for the last five months without a day off, and Jaheim had finally thought it was time to spend some money on them.

Tiny watched the white girl, Amber, switch her hips from left to right as they walked through the mall. She looked as if she was trying to catch a date, even on their day off. Jaheim had said that was one of the things he loved about her: the fact she was willing to work even when he was giving her a day off.

Amber had run away from home because she had gotten tired of the verbal and physical abuse her stepfather had subjected her to every time he got drunk. He had a habit of pulling her by her hair and viciously slapping her to the floor. Her mother had been married to him for three years. It had been the worst and longest three years of her young life.

On the day she had met Jaheim, she'd been contemplating hitchhiking to California where her biological father was incarcerated. He had about six months of his sentence left, and Amber wanted to be there once he was released. She had even considered taking her sister, Megan, along with her because their stepfather would surely begin in on her. Amber was tired of the abuse and even more sickened by how her mother turned a blind eye to what took place in their home.

By the time Jaheim approached her at the lakefront, she was ready to either run or end her own life. He had said all the right words to feed her emptiness, and in return her sole purpose in life was to please him. She was down to do any and everything he said, just like Brandy, and that bothered Tiny. Deep down she knew those females were willing to do things she wasn't, and she knew it was causing her to lose her man, a man she had basically given up her life and future for. She felt she had to do whatever it took to hold on to him because in the end he was really all she had.

"Tiny, you okay down there, momma? You ain't said a word the whole time we been in here. What, you sick or something?" Jaheim asked, sounding concerned.

She smile weakly. "Yeah, baby, I'm good. I just got a lot on my mind, that's all." She went to wrap her arm around his waist, but found Brandy had already stolen that spot. This irritated her more and more because it was beginning to seem as if Brandy was stealing her slot. All of the little things she used to do for Jaheim, Brandy managed to find a way to always beat her to the punch. She stole all of his affection, and he paid more attention to her than anyone else. It was causing her to become more and more jealous.

***

They were seated inside Ms. Bunch's Southern Home Cooking restaurant, halfway through their meal when Brandy reached over with a napkin and wiped ketchup from Jaheim's lip, then smiled and kissed him on the cheek.

Tiny dropped her fork right on top of her baked macaroni and cheese. "Damn, Brandy, don't you think you should leave me room to be able to wipe my man's mouth? You're acting like you're more his woman and not his sister. Bitch, you need to check yo'self, for real," Tiny said, preparing to jump across the table.

Brandy looked shocked. "Wow, my bad, Tiny. I ain't mean nothing by it. I just saw it there, and I went into action. I feel like he is a reflection of us, so we can't have him looking all out of place. I didn't mean to disrespect you, sis."

Now Tiny found herself feeling all uneasy. She started to think maybe the girl didn't know she was overstepping her bounds. After all, Jaheim never said anything ill to her about it. Maybe she was overreacting.

She was getting ready to apologize when Jaheim spoke up. "Tiny, stay in your lane. Don't be telling none of my women what not to do for me. If you were quicker on your toes, then maybe you would have saw it and got it before she did. You can't get mad at her because she on point and you're not."

Brandy was about to say something to defuse the bomb that was building between them, but decided to hold her peace. Jaheim leaned over, kissed her on the cheek, and smiled, wrapping his arm around her neck. He knew that would make

Amber continued to pick at the food she had barely touched. She was so self-conscious about her weight, even though at 5 feet, 4 inches tall she was only 110 pounds. She felt all blondes were supposed to be skinny, so she tried to stay on top of that, because her mother and grandmother were big girls. Also, for a seemingly small chick, she was blessed with a nice-sized bubble butt that caused most of her tricks to go insane.

She hated whenever Tiny and Jaheim got to fighting, and secretly didn't understand why they even needed Tiny around. She felt she and Brandy were carrying the load, and Tiny was just dead weight. She never listened, and she wanted to argue about everything. The only thing she had going for herself was the fact she was beautiful with a flawless yellow body.

"Jaheim, you know what? Maybe you're right. Maybe I should stay in my own lane. Go ahead, and you just keep on doing you. Like they say, every dog does have their day." She smiled and started to eat her food again.

"Yeah, and you better believe it, 'cause right now I'm howling at the muthafucking moon."

Brandy giggled and snuggled deeper into his embrace as two men walked in wearing enough jewelry to give Mr. T a run for his money. They saw Jaheim, nodded in his direction, then slowly began to make their way over to the table where he was seated. He wrapped his arms around Tiny and Brandy and looked up at the men, who looked down on him, not amused.

Tiny noted she vaguely recognized one of the younger men from their old high school. She had always thought he was fairly attractive and one of the best dressers there. She also liked the fact he had a deep chocolate complexion and dimples in each of his cheeks.

As soon as they got to the table, her and his eyes met. She immediately lowered hers, not wanting to seem like she was choosing, though she clearly felt like doing so.

"Yo, what's up, Jaheim? Can we talk to you outside for a minute?" the heavyset caramel-skinned man asked him, while at the same time looking around the restaurant as if he was sizing up witnesses.

Jaheim swallowed hard. "What's up, Joe? Anything y'all got to holler at me about, y'all can holler at me right here in front of my people. I ain't got nothing to hide from them," he said, fidgeting slightly in his seat.

The older woman behind the counter who had served them their food began to stare heavily in their direction while she poured an elderly man his coffee.

"Say, nigga, this strictly business. This ain't got nothing to do with these ladies. Matter of fact, I think it would be wise for you women to leave that booth before we turn this muthafucka into the fourth of July," the fat man said, already putting his hand under his shirt.

The other male, whom Tiny knew was called Savant, took the fat man's cue and put his hand under his shirt as well. "Look, I really ain't into splashing no females, but in about five seconds if y'all don't leave this nigga's side, I'm gon' have to look at y'all as casualties of war." At saying this, he looked directly into Tiny's eyes, almost pleaded with her to take heed of his warnings.

"Come on, Al, man, what the fuck y'all getting ready to hit me up for? I ain't did shit," Jaheim whined, looking around the restaurant for the best escape route.

Fat Al laughed. "Nigga, you know what it is. You done had two months to pay back what you owe, yet you still running around here trying to dodge the nation. Yo' interest done ran through the roof. That's 15 thousand total now, and unless you got that on you right now, my orders are to kill yo' ass on sight. I see you – so, nigga, either you pay or we follow the orders we been given."

Jaheim began looking around in a state of panic, and because he was starting to panic, the girls started to get uneasy. They looked back and forth at each other, and each had the fear of death in their eyes.

"You mean to tell me you about to kill me in here in front of all of these people?" Jaheim screamed, obviously trying to get everyone's attention who weren't sitting at the table.

The lady who was pouring the coffee wiped her hands on her apron and spoke up. "Look, y'all gon' have to get out of here with all of that mess. Take that shit outside. We're trying to run a business in here," she scolded with one hand on her hip. "I know y'all don't want me calling the police, because my husband works on the force, and if I call him down her all y'all asses going to jail. That goes for you hos, too. I'm sure y'all got warrants for something."

Savant put his hands in the air. "Say, hold up, lady. We ain't gotta go through all that. We don't need you calling the police and shit; at least, I don't. So, what we gon' do is we gon' respectfully leave your establishment." He turned and looked down at Jaheim. "Let's go, homey. Come on outside and take this shit like a man."

"I'm giving all y'all until the count of ten to pay your bill and get the fuck out of my place. If that does not happen, my husband about to be all up and through here, and a bunch of people going to jail. One. Two. Three."

Al scrunched up his face and gave Jaheim the look of death. "So, you gon' play pussy, huh? You go' go out like this? Alright then, your time coming, nigga. You get a pass today, but I promise you your time is coming. Come on, Savant. Let's get up out this bitch place before we be down in Cook County."

"Yeah, big homie, you right. We'll catch this nigga on the rebound, and I would advise you ladies to not be with him," he said, eyeing Tiny specifically.

She gave him a knowing look and then lowered her head.

"Four. Five. Six. Seven," the lady continued to count at the top of her lungs. She already had the telephone in her hands in a threatening gesture. "Y'all think it's a game, huh?"

Al slapped Savant on the back. "Come on, man,

let's bounce." They both took off out of the store, jumped into the Jeep they came in, and peeled away from the curb as if they knew the woman meant business.

As soon as they drove away, Jaheim stood up, waving his hands through the air. "Thanks, Alice, you saved my ass again. I thought they was about to body me. I owe you for this one."

She slammed the phone down and shook her head. "Yeah, well, you do owe me, but I ain't expecting you to pay me back, especially if you got dudes that's trying to kill you and you still ain't even paid them back. Boy, what have you went and got yourself into now? You know I'm telling your mother, right? As soon as I lock these doors down for the night, I'm calling her and I'm telling her on your li'l black ass. Then we gon' pray for you in church, and pray to Jesus we don't be burying you any time soon. Lord knows you are too young to die, but you're also too stupid to know that. You running around here thinking you're pimping these little girls when all along the devil is pimping you. You need to turn away from your sins, Jaheim. You are breaking your mother's heart. And you harlots need to find a new profession, or at least a new pimp, because y'all gon' get my nephew killed. Now, y'all get out of here before those thugs come back and shoot my place up. I just wax them floors, and I don't feel like mopping up no damn blood. My back already hurting. Boy, come on and pay this bill and get y'all ass out of here," the fat old lady said, taking a napkin and wiping the sweat off her forehead.

***

"Girl, you sure you're okay? You been in that bathroom all day long. I know you ain't got diarrhea that bad, so what's going on?" Amber questioned through the crack of the door.

Tiny was on the other side freaking out. She was waiting for the third pregnancy test to reveal its results. The first two had already come back positive, and she was praying the third would come back anything but that.

"Amber, I'm good. I'm just going through something right now. I'll be out there in a minute." She took a towel from the rack and wet it with cold water, running it across her face. She could not believe this was happening. She was not ready to raise a child. She found herself so deep within the lifestyle that nothing else mattered other than appeasing Jaheim, especially since he had picked up two more women. The competition was getting fierce, and since she was the oldest female, she felt she would eventually wind up being on the losing end.

She felt the bile rising in the back of her throat again and slumped to her knees over the toilet, regurgitating her entire lunch. After flushing, she pressed her forehead against the cool bowl and said a silent prayer to the heavens, asking God to please make her not be pregnant. None of that made a difference, because she picked up the stick and her greatest fear was confirmed for the third time.

"Fuck, fuck, fuck! I ask for one little thing, one

simple thing, God, and you can't even do that for me? What have I ever done to you to make you crap all over me like this? Now what am I going to do, Lord?" she whimpered, dropping back to her knees and sobbing.

There were three loud knocks on the door, followed by Jaheim's booming voice. "Tiny, open this damn door right now or I'm about to kick this bitch down!" he threatened.

"Boy, calm down. I'm good. I'm just taking care of something right now," Tiny said faintly, feeling so weak she could barely move.

"I ain't ask you how you were feeling, I told you to open this muthafucking door. Now do like I ask you, or this bitch coming down!"

"Tiny, please open the door before he get all crazy," Brandy yelled.

"Girl, shut up and take yo ass back in the room. This ain't got nothing to do with you."

"But I was just trying to—"

"You heard what the fuck I said, now get!"

Tiny heard the girl's footsteps descend the hallway, then the knocking started all over again.

"Tiny, open this damn door!"

Tiny lay on the floor, oblivious to his threats. She just didn't care anymore. If he wanted to break a door down, then so be it. The door was barely hanging on as it was. She decided she was going to lay on the floor until he made his move. Whatever happened would happen.

Before she could even finish her thoughts, there was a loud boom and the door flew inward. She still did not move. She stayed in the middle of the floor with roaches crawling around her and allowed her mind to drift away to a far, distant land where her reality did not exist. A place where there were no such things as project buildings, rats, roaches, starvation, pimps, or hos.

When she came back to reality, Jaheim was lifting her by her hair and growling into her face. "Bitch, you mean to tell me you allowed yourself to become pregnant? How the fuck did yo' stupid ass do that?" he spat recklessly into her face.

"Jaheim, leave me the fuck alone. I don't feel like going through this with you right now. I'm trying to decide what I'm getting ready to do."

"What you getting ready to do? Bitch, you know what you getting ready to do. You about to take your ass up there to 115 and Indiana Avenue and get an abortion. We ain't got no room to be raising no muthafucking kids. So get ready. This money I'm about to waste on this stupid stunt you just pulled, you gon' work day and night until I get it back, then you make up for the time you lost getting that money back when you should have been hustling along with the rest of the girls for our first cause. So, bitch, you gon' be behind for a minute, but in the end it's gon' all make sense. I'm gon' make sure of that."

Tiny acted as if she could not hear the rap he was spitting. She had not made her mind up, and she wasn't completely sold on killing her baby just because he thought it would be a good idea. She felt trapped in more ways than one.

"Get your ass up and let's go," he said, reaching for her hand.

"No."

"Bitch, what you just say?"

She jerked away from him, fell to her knees, and hurled into the toilet again, retching her guts for far longer than she had before. After she finished, she wet the towel again and ran it across her face. "Jaheim, I said no. I'm not about to kill my baby just because you think it's a good idea. You ain't got no type of heart. Don't you know you're the only person I screw without protection, so the only person's baby this is would be yours?" she said, then fell back to her knees, dry heaving.

"Mine? What the fuck you mean, mine? Bitch, you out there fucking every nigga in Chicago, and even a few that ain't from this muhfucka, and you got the audacity to say some stupid shit like that? Get yo' dumb ass up and let's go take care of that bastard inside of you. I'm not gon' ask you again."

Tiny spit into the toilet. "Boy, fuck you. I ain't going nowhere, so now what you gon' do?"

"What I'm gon' do? What I'm gon' do? Did you just ask me that?" he said, slipping his belt out of his pants and whipping it across the air until it landed across the back of her neck. He swung it again, and this time it crashed onto her back, causing her to holler out in pain, but this only infused his rage. He proceeded to beat her as if she was an unruly child while she curled into a ball, protecting her stomach. When she felt him dragging her across the floor by her hair and into the living room, she knew she'd had enough. She simply could not take it anymore.

"Alright, Jaheim, alright. I'm so sorry. I'll

listen, baby. Please forgive me, I'll listen."

He picked her up by her hair and stared into her face. "That's right, bitch. You betta, because I'm tired of playing games with you. Now you gon' take this money and take yo' punk-ass down to that clinic and get that issue taken care of. And if I have to go through this shit with you one more time, I swear to God I'm gon' kill you. Do you hear me?"

She nodded. "Yeah, daddy, loud and clear."

Chapter 4

Tiny looked around the waiting room in the small clinic and felt like the air was being sucked out of her lungs. As she stepped to the desk, a heavyset Asian woman handed her a clipboard and gave her the phoniest smile known to man. Everything about the atmosphere screamed wrong.

"Chu take form and chu fill out ober dare. I call chu name when chu done and know what chu here for, undastan'?"

Tiny smiled. "Yeah, I understand you." She sat back down and began to fill the forms out. With each question she answered, tears began to well up in her eyes. She was trying to make sense of everything: how she had gotten there, and how she would get out of the hole she was trapped in. She started to feel sick to her stomach again.

Before she knew the time had elapsed, she had given the woman back the forms and her name was being called.

"Mizz Johnson, kin take chu now. Chu you come on and go wiff me."

Tiny followed the chubby lady down the narrow hallway until she directed her inside a small room with a patient's bed and stirrups. The lady then took her blood pressure and temperature.

"The doc will be in in a minute. Chu stay put and don't take nuffin'. I watch chu." She wagged her finger at her, then turned and stepped out of the room.

Tiny couldn't help but laugh. The little woman was kind of funny. She looked around the room for something to steal anyway, and after finding nothing of value, she decided to stuff some alcohol pads into her purse. She sat back and began reading the posters covering the small room. Most of them scared her because they spoke about incurable diseases and the deterioration of the body due to those diseases. She felt a cold shiver run through her.

"Hello, Miss Johnson," a tall, dark-skinned, balding man said while stepping into the room. He sat down in the chair across from her and read over the clipboard her forms were plastered on. He started to shake his head and kept repeating the words, "I see."

She began to fidget uncomfortably in her seat. It felt like the room was getting hotter and smaller at the same time. She started to wonder why she was there alone. Why hadn't Jaheim come down with her to support her through this ordeal? After all, he did have a hand in it, one way or the other. Even if he thought he wasn't the father, he was still responsible for putting her on the stroll every day. It was the law of cause and effect. How did he not understand that, she wondered.

"So, Ms. Johnson, it says here you are looking to have an abortion or to terminate your pregnancy. How far along do you think you are?"

She continued to fidget in her seat. "I don't know. I would say about nine weeks. My period is way past due."

"I see. And are you absolutely certain this is what you want to do?" He looked up from the forms with his glasses slightly lowered onto his nose.

She nodded her head slowly. "Yeah, I think so."

"Ms. Johnson, I apologize if I sound unsympathetic, but you have to be absolutely sure this is what you want. After all, this is your child, and you would be ending its life. You have to make sure you are certain, because this is not something you would want to regret down the line, ya know? It is not my job to tell you in which direction to go, but it is my job to make you aware of all your possible options."

Once again, she nodded her head slowly.

"Well?"

There was a long pause between them before Tiny looked up. "Huh? Well, what?"

"Well, are you absolutely sure? You didn't answer that question yet."

"I mean, I have no other choice."

"What about the father? Is he in the picture, or would you prefer not to discuss him in the matter?"

Tiny grunted, "The father is the reason I am here. He wants me to have an abortion." She felt the tears running down her face.

The doctor reached behind him and pulled out four tissues and handed them to her. "So I see, but what is it you want, exactly? I assume you still want to be with this man, so do you think killing your child will be enough to keep him?"

Tiny lowered her head, and the tears really began to pour down her cheeks. "I don't know. I don't know what it will take to please him anymore. I really don't want to kill my baby, but if I don't I feel like I'll lose him. And not only that, if I keep him he'll wind up killing me. Then, on the other hand, my lifestyle will not allow me to be a productive mother to this child. I'm just turning 18, and I have no idea what it will take to raise a kid. I'm so scared, and I feel so alone.

The doctor nodded his sympathies. "What is your relationship like with your parents?"

She shrugged her shoulders. "I don't know, I guess it could be better. I haven't seen them ever since I made the decision to leave home with this guy, and I have no idea how they are going to react to this pregnancy news. I don't want to hear their I-told-you-so's." She dropped her head and started to sob uncontrollably. It was like she really didn't understand what all she was up against until she said it out loud.

The doctor reached across and took her hand within his own. "Well, I think the first thing we should do is run some tests and get you an ultrasound to determine how far along you really are. Then we'll work on deciding what it is here you really want to do. I think it would be a great idea to get your parents involved, or maybe your church. Are you a member of a church?"

"Yes."

"Oh, yeah? Which one?"

"Mercy Memorial Baptist Church, over on 52nd and Sangament."

"Oh, yes. I am very familiar with Pastor Moore. That brother is deep. I am going to personally give him a call tonight and ask for his assistance, if that is okay with you. Maybe if you get a little more support, you'll find out your child is worth having. Okay?"

She nodded again.

"First, let's run some tests. I'll be right back."

***

Tiny left the clinic with a whole new frame of mind. She actually felt better and a bit more optimistic.

The sun had peeked out from behind the clouds, and the humidity was becoming unbearable. She had to walk two blocks to get to the proper bus stop, and started to hate Jaheim for not being there for her when she came out. He was so selfish, and so self-absorbed. She felt there was no way he could truly care about her, because if he did, he would not allow her to go through the things that happened. Not only that, he also would not be the culprit of taking her through 90 percent of the tribulations.

She started to fan her face as she made it to the bus stop. She looked down the busy street, trying to locate the bus, and felt irritated when she looked the other way and saw she had just missed it. She felt like only bad things were able to happen to her, like she was ineligible for happiness.

She fanned her face with a few of the pamphlets she had taken away from the clinic and prayed she wouldn't pass out right there on the busy street.

She was in the midst of talking to Jesus when she heard a loud horn beeping across the street, then a man calling her by her government name.

"Zivial! Zivial! Girl, I know you hear me calling you!"

She placed her hand over her face to shield the

sun, and also to get a better idea as to who it could have possibly been. All she could definitely make out was the loud music and the rapper Easy E's voice.

Whoever it was, she was about to find out real soon. Once she was able to make out the person who was calling her was driving an all-black, freshly waxed Corvette with gold Daytons, they were making a crazy and dangerous U-turn in the middle of the street. They floored the accelerator until they were fast coming up alongside the curb where she was standing.

She jumped back for fear of being run over, almost bumping into the old woman who had managed to creep up and take her place behind her in preparation to board the next bus. As soon as the window rolled down, her first thought was she was about to be assassinated for something Jaheim had done. She felt tingles going all through her body, and she braced herself for the flurry of bullets that were sure to come.

"Zivial, girl, stop playin'. Oh, what, you ignoring me now?" she heard the familiar voice say.

She opened her eyes one at a time and searched the occupant's face, then took a deep breath when it all started to make sense. "Meryl? Boy, fuck, you scared the shit out of me!" she said, placing a hand over her heart that was beating so fast it felt like it was trying to leap out of her chest.

He started to laugh and nod his head at the same time. "Let me guess, you still fucking with that shiesty-ass Jaheim, and that nigga got you thinking the whole Chicago out to kill y'all ass, huh?" He shook his head and laughed out loud again.

She lowered her own. "Yeah, well, you know how shit is. What's up with you, though? How have you been?"

He looked into his rear view mirror as a line of cars began to blow their horns for him to move on. He acted as if they didn't exist and turned his focus back onto her, turning his music down a few notches. "I'm good, trying my best to sew this hood up. I still think about your li'l yellow ass, and I hate how we parted."

The horn blowing behind his car was starting to get ridiculous. Tiny was worried in a few seconds somebody was going to pull a gun out and get to shooting. After all, it was Chicago. She wanted to say something, but didn't know how to respond to what he had just said.

They had dated for two years back in school, before she had ever gotten with Jaheim. Meryl was always so nice to her and treated her like a queen. His only problem was he was too nice, and during the NWA era everybody was searching for and trying to fall in love with a thug, and a thug he was not. He also wasn't in a rush to lay her on her back, and there was no secret she was hot blooded and needed a thug to put it down on her in the worst way all the time.

He didn't step up to the plate, and one day in the bathroom during study hall, when the yearning had gotten so bad she was finding herself rubbing her thighs together just to ease some of the throbbing in her jewel, Jaheim had suddenly appeared in the girls' bathroom, where he had snatched her up and threw her against the wall, ripped her panties from under her short skirt, and bent her over the sink and fucked her at full speed, forcing her to look at her own reflection in the mirror while he took her so savagely. All she could do was moan at the top of her lungs and think to herself they could be caught at any moment because the bathroom was unlocked.

Just thinking back on that first time had caused her nipples to spike, and she felt herself getting juicy.

She was snapped out of her zone by Meryl calling her name.

"What, huh?"

"I said get in, or you gon' wind up getting me shot. We got a whole lot of catching up to do." He opened the door.

"Alright, but you betta not try no funny business," she teased. She sat in the car and immediately felt like she was in Heaven as soon as the air conditioner hit her in the face. She looked around the car and noted the interior was all leather, and it felt so soft and soothing to her skin. "Damn, I see you doing good for yourself."

He smiled, reached, and switched the tape to Keith Sweat. "What, you thought I was gon' stay that same li'l awkward kid my whole life? I mean, I was a late bloomer, but now I get how this shit goes. I know what you females respond to. I didn't back then, but I get it now."

Tiny felt uneasy. "Say, Meryl, I'm sorry how that all went down. You know I was an immature girl trying to discover myself. You didn't do nothing wrong, that was all my fault. I wish I could go back and change the way I did you."

"Change how you did me?" He took a brief second to look over at her. "You straight. What you did was what you was supposed to do. It's because of you I hopped up off the porch and hit these streets hard. Oh, and don't be calling me by my government name, either. My name is Cash."

"My bad, Cash. But I do feel out of order, because back then we did have something good between us that I haven't been able to find ever since you."

She watched as he sped through a yellow light, almost clipping a brown van that was making an illegal left turn. At seeing that, she reached to her side and strapped her seatbelt across her body.

"That shit history. You live and you learn." He took a blunt from behind his ear and pushed in the car lighter. "You smoke?"

"Yeah, I dabble a little bit. Why, you gon' let me smoke with you?" she flirted.

He smiled, his handsome face lighting up. "I got you, girl. Where you was on your way to? And more importantly, what nigga you fucking with got you riding on a bus? I know you ain't fell off like that?" He took a long pull from the blunt. The smoke came out in thick clouds, surrounding the car.

"I was on my way to the Stateways, and I'm still fucking with Jaheim." She said this last part almost embarrassed to do so.

"Yeah, I figured that," he said, handing her the blunt.

She took it and pulled on the cigar that was

rolled so fat it was as if it had never been bussed down to begin with. The smoke was so harsh it caused her to break into a fit of coughs. He reached over and began slapping her on the back. She rolled down the window to try and get some more air into her lungs, but al she was met with was the scorching heat and humidity. "Damn, what the fuck you got rolled up in here?" she said through a cracking voice, rolling the window back up because it was giving her no relief whatsoever.

"That's that good-good. What, y'all ain't blowing Purple Haze over there in the Stateways yet?"

She beat her fist on her chest as she felt the high taking over her mind. "I guess not, because I ain't never tasted nothing like that." All at once, all of the feelings of her being became sensitive and highly erotic. Without even knowing what she was doing, she began to rub her hand over her thick thigh, causing her short skirt to ascend.

Cash smiled and licked his lips. He looked down and saw her skirt had risen almost to the point it was sitting in her lap. He could just begin to make out the red lace panties. The car began to slowly veer into the wrong lane. He was brought back to reality when a car blew its horn.

Tiny continued to rub all over her thighs. She felt her nipples harden, and they felt so alive under her halter. She was glad she had neglected to wear a bra; it gave her B cups freedom. She started to rub her thighs together to extinguish some of the flames shooting off inside of her.

"You know what? It's a beautiful day outside.

Why don't we swing over on Lakeshore Drive and see the water? You cool with that?"

She smiled and licked her lips as he passed her the blunt again.

As soon as they were parked, Cash turned to her in his seat. "You know what, Zivial? You did do me wrong back then. Don't you feel like you owe me an apology?" he asked, placing a hand on her thick thigh.

Tiny arched her back at the feel of his touch. Her nipples started to throb, and she inadvertently spread her thighs, giving him room for his hand to travel wherever it pleased.

There were other parked cars around them, along with some families outside barbequing, enjoying the sunny day. They paid no attention to the surrounding melee.

"Oh yeah? Well, what kind of apology did you have in mind?"

He smiled. "I don't know, but we can definitely think of something," he said, now rubbing all over the front of her panties.

She took her left foot and raised it until it was flat on the seat, then she reached to the side of her seat and released the lever that allowed her chair to recline some.

Cash wasted no time sliding his fingers under her leg band and directly onto her basement's lips. He felt the moisture and heard her growl deep within her throat. She spread her legs even farther apart.

"Damn. I wouldn't have known what to do with all of this back then, but I bet you I know what to do with it now."

He slid his fingers into her body, and Tiny leaned over and bit into his neck as she felt him darting into her again and again.

***

When it was all said and done, she had given him the best head she could muster, making it real sloppy the way she knew so many men liked it. Then she rode him reverse cowgirl-style, holding his ankles and making sure he paid attention to her ass as it bounced and separated for him.

He actually had the nerve to clean her with his tongue afterward, vacuuming all of their sexual secretion. She couldn't believe he had managed to leave her twisted. Whoever had taught him had taught him good. She wanted to make sure they didn't lose contact with one another ever again.

"Alright, you can take the rest of this pizza upstairs with you. And you got my pager number. You make sure you call me whenever you ready to leave dude's ass, or whenever you want to get together and repeat today's performance, you hear me?"

She nodded. "Yeah, I hear you." She reached into his lap and squeezed his dick, then leaned down and kissed it through his shorts. "I'm definitely gon' be in touch."

He smiled. "Oh, and here, take this weed with you. I got plenty of this shit." He reached under his seat and came back up with an ounce. "That's you right there. Give me kiss."

She kissed his lips and felt him rub all over her ass, even taking time out to slip his fingers into her. After they broke their embrace, he stuck them into his mouth. She wanted to take him right there all over again.

When she got back into the apartment, there was no one there, so she sat the pizza on the table and ran herself a hot bath. After locking the door, she settled into the tub, closed her eyes, and replayed the events that just took place. Before she knew it, her leg was over the side of the tub and her fingers danced beneath the water.

T.J. & Jelissa

Chapter 5

"Tiny! Tiny! Bitch, wake yo' ass up. Did you go take care of that business like I told you to?"

"What? Damn, Jaheim, leave me the fuck alone. Don't you see me in here trying to get some sleep?" she whined, sick because he had disrupted her dreams of Cash.

"Bitch, I don't give a fuck about you getting no sleep. Now answer my muthafucking question! Did you go down there yesterday and take care of that business like I asked you to?"

Tiny ripped the sheets from her body and sat up in the pullout bed. "Ugh, damn, you so fucking stupid. What, you thought they was gon' take the baby out of me on the first day? I have to make an appointment for that procedure, and they will only allow me to make that appointment after they confirm I am pregnant. All they did yesterday was run some tests, and the doctor said he would be back at me very soon with the results. And for the record, yeah, Jaheim, I am doing fine. I found a way to make it home all by myself, even though I felt weak the whole time." She rolled her eyes and stood before him in the nude. She reached onto the floor and grabbed her gown, first shaking the roaches off of it and giving it a thorough once over before sliding it over her body.

Brandy came to the bedroom door in a see-through negligee. She walked in and planted a kiss onto Jaheim's cheek. "Good morning, daddy. Did you sleep well?"

He wrapped his arm around her and kissed her

on the forehead. "Yeah, it was good. Now, go'n back in there while I deal with this bitch."

On the way out he slapped her on her thick behind, causing her to yelp.

"Anyway, back to you, bitch. I know that if two months from now yo' punk-ass get to showing any type of sign of pregnancy, I'm gon' kick you and that baby ass. I ain't ready for no kids, especially no whore baby. You got that?"

"Yeah, I got you real good," she said, feeling her throat go tight and her eyes begin to mist over.

"Alright, just as long as we got an understanding, then there won't be no consequences. Let me know when you gon' need the money, and until then you gon' get your ass out there and work just like everybody else." He walked past her and gave her a slight bump. He was halfway out of the room when he paused in the doorway. "And where the fuck you get some money from to buying pizza and shit? Where the change at?"

"What?"

"The pizza, bitch. The pizza that's in the living room. Where you get the money from to buy that, and where is the change from it?"

Tiny gave him a disgusted look. "Jaheim, stop playing with me, for real. Get the fuck out of here and go tend to them bitches in the living room. You asking me about some fucking pizza, and I would have been starving for two whole days if I didn't manage to get that. Stop playing with me, for real."

He frowned up his face, looked down the hallway, then stepped into the room and closed the door. "That ain't no answer. I asked you where you got that shit from, and you still ain't told me that. Now answer my question."

She ignored him. She walked to the dresser and searched through it until she found a pair of panties and a bra. She then picked out a tight, body-hugging summer dress and made her way to the bathroom with him following close behind.

"Tiny, you think I'm playing with you, don't you?" he said, smacking her on the back of the head.

She turned around and in one slick motion slapped him directly across the face, taking him off guard, then she lunged forward and kicked him in the nuts, dropping him to his knees.

"I'm tired of you putting your dirty-ass hands on me. I'm sick of your shit."

She went to kick him again, but was tackled to the floor by Amber.

"Get off of my daddy, you stupid bitch! What's the matter with you?" she screamed into Tiny's face, pinning her to the floor.

"Oh, bitch, I know you didn't." Tiny struggled to get from under her. As soon as she got her bearings, she stood and punched her square in the nose, causing blood to squirt all over her shirt. Amber put both hands up to her face, covering it, and the girls watched as blood leaked through her fingers.

Tiny was thinking about hitting her again when she felt someone jump onto her back.

"Leave my sister alone, you black, crazy bitch! She didn't do anything to you!"

"Get off of me, tramp! Get the fuck off of my back and fight me head-up. I'm about to whoop you and your sister ass."

She flung Amber's little sister to the floor and then jumped on top of her, slapping her again and again. Out of the corner of her eye, she could see Jaheim starting to gather himself, and she started to grow worried. She pushed Megan to the floor and stood up.

"Look, everybody, just leave me alone. I don't want to fight any of you. Jaheim, my mom bought me that pizza. I'm sorry, baby. Please forgive me."

He struggled to get to his feet. Once there, he walked over to her and backhanded her, sending her flying against the wall. The punishment didn't end until Jaheim had all the girls take belts and beat her for a full 10 minutes.

An hour later, she was on the track.

***

"Our Father, who are in Heaven, hallowed be thy name. Thy Kingdom come, may thy will be done on Earth as it is in Heaven. Give us this day our daily bread, and forgive us our trespasses as we forgive those who trespass against us. And lead us not into temptation, but deliver us from evil. For thine is the Kingdom, the power, and the glory, forever and ever. Amen."

Tiny knelt down in the front of the pew with her hands clasped in front of her. She felt the tears dripping down her cheeks and the lump in her throat. She took a deep breath. "Dear God, I pray you have mercy on my soul. I pray you forgive me for my sins, and you provide a way for me to be able to step away from them. For what am I if I am nothing within your sight? I beg of you for strength and the determination to become a better me. Give me an outlet. Please, Father. I ask these things and all things within your holy and precious name. Through the vessel of Jesus I pray. Amen."

She took another deep breath and stood up, wiping her face. All around her people were doing the same thing. Pastor Moore had just finished delivering a touching sermon about forgiving themselves, a sermon that had touched Tiny like never before. She felt so lost and abandoned. She had come to church seeking direction, and secretly a glimpse of her family. Her mother sat only two rows over from her and didn't even acknowledge her presence. That had hurt her more than anything, but she decided she wouldn't allow that to deter her from what she had previously planned. So she dusted her knees off and ran her fingers through her flowing weave and walked over to her mother, who sat with a Bible in her lap, reading over the gospels.

"Hey, Momma. Long time, no see," she whispered, sliding in and sitting down next to her.

She curled up the side of her face and started to fan herself with the paper fan the ushers had handed out as they walked through the door. "I'm surprised to see you here. I would have thought a whore would burn up in church." She laughed at her own joke. "You come to steal money from the collection plate or something? Or you hoping they giving out free food?"

Tiny had to bite her tongue. It wasn't unusual for her mother to behave in this fashion. For as long as she could remember, her mother had always treated her worse than all of her siblings, and she never understood why.

"Momma, how are you?"

She continued to read her Bible, refusing to look up and address her daughter. "I can tell you one thing, I'm doing better than you. I'm still with the same man I been with. I bet that's something you can't say."

"How is my father, and my sisters?"

For the first time she looked up at her daughter. "Girl, why? Ain't nobody asking about you. Mind your own damn business!" She wiped her forehead with a handkerchief. "Here you go, got me cursing all in church, losing my religion."

"Momma, I think that I may be pregnant, and I don't know what to do. I'm scared."

Her mother continued to fan herself. When she started to shake her head. Tiny knew she was about to make a whole lot of slick comments that wouldn't do anything to help her situation. It would only make her feel a whole lot worse.

For as long as she could remember, her mother had always looked down on her and treated her as if she were a step-child and she herself was Mommy Dearest. Through it all she had still managed to find a way to love her mother deep within her heart, and she had never fit her mouth to say anything disrespectful toward her. A part of her felt like her mother secretly had high hopes for her, and she had let her down, and this was her mother's way of lashing out. Either way, it hurt Tiny's feelings more than she could ever admit. She always thought it was her mother's job to be there to protect and nurture her — two jobs she felt that her mom had dropped the ball on.

She was really starting to have second thoughts about showing up to church that day. She began to silently scold herself.

Her mother curled up the side of her face and gave her a sinister smile. She scooted over closer to her and leaned into her ear. "So, you finally having Satan's baby? Well, ain't that just something. You been out there parading around like the whore of Babylon, and you thought you wasn't gon' eventually bring home a little devil? You're a tart, and I ain't sorry for you. Don't think you about to bring your little ass back into my home and be all up under my man." She began shaking her head like a menace. "Un-uh, that ain't gon' happen. You can bet your bottom dollar on that."

One of the sisters of the church started to come down the aisle in their direction with a hat so big it was like she was wearing an umbrella on her head.

"Ooh, here come Sister Jefferies right now. You best not say nothing to her about your situation. I'm already embarrassed enough with you walking in here like you just left a strip club. Damn, I don't know where I went wrong with you," she said, frowning.

"Sister Johnson, how are you, dear?" the old woman said, trying to balance the big hat on her neck. She looked as if she was having a hard time.

"Hello, sister. Well, I'm just doing fine. I feel

blessed, and I know the good Lord has me on His radar, so I stay in prayer like it has me trapped," Tiny's mother said, ducking under the big hat to give the woman a hug.

They wrapped their arms around each other and tried to kiss one another on the cheek, but only wound up knocking their heads together. Tiny couldn't help but giggle a little to herself.

"And Lord, don't tell me that's Zivial! Girl, look at yo' small self, looking all yellow and beautiful. It seems like just yesterday you were in the youth choir, terrified to do your solo. Now look at you standing there, looking like a little woman. You better give me a hug." She opened up her arms so wide she hit a man on the back who stood talking to a woman the next aisle over. He turned around and smiled at them, and she apologized.

Tiny walked up to her, ducked under the hat, and gave her a hug. The woman smelled as if she had bathed herself in perfume and vanilla. She slapped Tiny on the back, and then hugged her again. Tiny started to feel a bit uncomfortable, especially when the woman kissed her on the cheek. She tried to wiggle out of her embrace, but she held her.

"Sister Johnson, I'm telling you this one right here is going to be something great. This girl is going to make God proud. You just wait, I can feel it coming through her. She is meant for greatness." She hugged Tiny tighter and then let her go.

Tiny's mother smirked. "Yeah, girl, I hope you right. I don't know if I'm going to hold my breath, though. You know, I wouldn't want to put too much pressure on her."

"Well, I think you should put all the pressure on her that God musters inside of you. You are the parent, and He knows what it's going to take in order to get her where she needs to be. Don't worry about the pressure. And you, Zivial, all you do is follow your heart. God has a plan for you, little woman. I'm telling you what I know, and I feel it in you when I hug you."

Tiny felt like she was burning up all the sudden. It felt like someone had pushed her into an oven and turned the knob to broil. She didn't know how to respond to the woman. She had not even thought about what she wanted to do with her life as of yet, and a part of her felt like she had thrown her dreams away the day she chose Jaheim over her schooling. The only thing she felt she had left that meant anything to her was her notebook full of poetry. It was her oasis.

She decided to nod her head. "I thank you for that, sister, and I'm going to do everything I can to fulfill the mission he has for me." Tiny didn't know what she was saying. All she wanted to do was get from in front of the old woman, because her mother was giving her a look that said she was not impressed and a little bit irritated.

Tiny thought she would faint when she saw her father making his way over to them. He had taken his suit coat off, and there were large sweat stains under his arms. The side of his face had sweat rivulets pouring down them, and he looked beyond annoyed. He walked directly up to her mother without acknowledging her or Mrs. Jefferies.

"Woman, it is time to go. I don't understand why every time church let out you gotta walk around and mingle with all these people. Jesus done saw us come, now we can leave," he said, wiping sweat from his forehead.

"Hi, Daddy," Tiny said with her eyes pinned on the floor.

He frowned and looked down at her. "Girl, hi. Now you come on, let's go," he said, walking off and out of the church.

"Well, I guess I'll see you ladies later. Y'all take care, and may the Lord continue to be a force within your lives. God bless."

Tiny watched as her mother followed behind her father. It had always been that way. She could not remember a time when her mother stood up for herself or had her own voice when it came to him.

Her father was a cruel man. He had very little respect for her mother, and he treated her as if she were expendable. In fact, he also treated her and her siblings the same way. The only thing she could ever remember him cherishing in life was the bottle. Her father would do anything for a shot of alcohol, and when he didn't have it all hell was sure to break loose, so Tiny's mother made sure he always had it and that it wasn't a problem.

She and her father never got along because, to her, he was simply too abusive. She had sustained the worst beatings and injuries from his hands, and even sometimes weapons. Her father did not care how he inflicted pain, just as long as he inflicted it.

"Well, sister Zivial, I guess it's just you and me. Where are you living now? I thought you was getting ready to leave with them, but it look like they done left you behind. Are you okay?" she whispered.

Tiny nodded her head, but didn't feel okay in the least bit. Sister Jefferies gave her a look that said she wasn't convinced. She turned and looked toward the front of the church. "Before you leave, I want you to go and give the pastor a hug. I make sure I do that every Sunday, and sister, I gotta tell you my week is always blessed. So, from Sunday to Sunday the Lord walks with me, and all I gotta do is get my blessing renewed on his day. Come on, sister." She reached and grabbed Tiny's hand.

Tiny followed behind her as if she were a little girl being led by her mother.

The church was beginning to become empty. There were only about 12 people left who were still hugging and saying their goodbyes.

When they got to the front of the church, the pastor was just finishing up hugging two of the deacons. He slapped them on the backs, and told them he couldn't wait to see them at revival the following week. They promised to be there, and then the two heavyset men made their way to their awaiting wives and families.

As soon as they were out of the way, sister Jefferies was taking her hat off and wrapping her arms around the Denzel Washington look-alike, catching him by surprise.

"Pastor, I'm here for my blessing, and I pray to God he works through you and directly onto me. I need your healing, and I need for you to keep me safe through the week. Lord knows the city of

Chicago getting worse and worse, and I'm starting to fear for my life on a daily basis."

The Pastor nodded his head. "Sister, don't you worry." He wrapped his arms around her and began to pray over her, loud enough for only her to hear him.

After he finished, the sister hugged him again and came and pulled Tiny by the arm. "Pastor, this here is Zivial and Timmy's daughter. She came today because she need a blessing and a word from God. I told her God works miracles through you, and she needed you to lay hands on her. Hallelujah!"

Tiny continued to stare at the ground, so embarrassed. She wondered why the woman had to make her feel so stupid in front of the handsome reverend. She would have given anything to have not been there in that instant.

"Is this true, little sister?" he asked, wrapping his arm around her shoulders.

Tiny nodded shyly, still refusing to take her eyes away from the ground. That was her safest bet, to not make eye contact with him. She felt if she did, he would see who she really was and what her spirit was really like.

She felt him hold her tighter. "Sister, you never have to be shy when you are in God's house, for it is here where you can come as you are and not be judged. Everybody in this place is with sin; none of us are worthy to cast stones. The most important thing is that you are here, and you are ready to give the Lord his due, ask him for his forgiveness, and seek his love. Am I right?"

"Yes, sir." She felt the sweat starting to run down her back.

"Well, I'm gon' let you two go ahead. My husband ready to go. Zivial, you take care, sweetie. I will see you next Sunday. God bless the both of you, and thank you, pastor," she said, putting the big hat back on.

The Pastor grabbed Tiny's hand and led her out of the sanctuary. She followed him downstairs and into where she knew his office was. Once there, he closed the door and took off his suit jacket.

"Sister, I know exactly who you are. I received a call from a dear friend of mine a few days ago, and he told me about your situation. I was looking for the right time to be able to approach you, and Lord I'm glad sister Jefferies was there to bring you to me." He loosened his tie. "So, how are you doing?"

Tiny felt blindsided. She had forgotten all about the doctor and what he had promised to do for her. Now that she sat across from the pastor and the situation was thrust upon her, she felt at a loss for words. She started to fidget in her seat, and suddenly the air-conditioned room was not cool enough.

"I don't know. I guess I'm a little scared and still undecided as to what I want to do." She crossed her thighs and tried her best to pull the short skirt down some. When she noticed it was halfway up her thighs, she thought about uncrossing her legs and pulling it back down, but then she got to feeling self-conscious and wondered what it would look like to do that in front of the pastor. She could feel his eyes glued to her face, so she tried her best to not show any signs of discomfort. Every time she moved, she felt her skirt rise a little more.

"And have you spoken with your parents about this ordeal?"

Tiny nodded her head. "I just brought it up to my mother out there, and she seemed as if she didn't want any parts of it. She said it was Satan's baby, and I was a harlot, and what was I supposed to expect? I just don't know what to do," she whimpered, and for the first time noticed she was crying. She couldn't understand how she had managed to let her guard down so easily.

The pastor seemed to fly from around the desk, dropping to his knees and wrapping his arms around her shoulders. "It's ok, little sister. I need you to know you are not alone, and everything is going to be okay."

She continued to sob and rock back and forth within his arms.

"Sister, where are you staying? Are you living with your parents, or what is your situation?"

She didn't know if she should tell him the truth, or simply try to save face. She wondered how she could face the man if he found out she was living with her dope fiend pimp. For some reason she didn't want him to look down on her, but at the same time she felt he was actually trying to help her better her situation. She decided she would follow that little voice within.

"I am currently living in the Stateway Projects with a few friends. It's not the best arrangement, but it is all I have."

The pastor looked up from his knees. "The Stateways? There were just three murders there last night, and the night before there were two, and three women were raped and nearly killed. That's nonsense." He jumped to his feet and picked up the phone. "Me and my wife are blessed to have a big home. There is no one there other than our daughter, who will be going to college in the fall. You are more than welcome to stay with us until you get back on your feet. I'm going to talk this over with my wife and give you a few days. On Tuesday, I want you to meet me here at 9:00 p.m. Our revival will be just letting out, and you'll be coming and moving in with us. Do you hear me, young lady? I refuse to take no for an answer." He gave her a look that said he meant business.

Tiny felt like the decision was already made for her, so all she could do was nod her head. "Yes, sir."

T.J. & Jelissa

Chapter 6

That night, Tiny had a hard time sleeping. She tossed and turned and threw all of the sheets off the bed. She could not believe what the pastor was willing to do for her. She was already resigned to the notion she would be doing everything on her own, but now that she had a person other than herself who was willing to step up to the plate and help her, she felt it brought on a new ambiance.

No matter how hard she tried, she could not fall asleep. She remembered her father's sister Gwen, her favorite aunt, always told her if she was ever having trouble getting to sleep, she should drink warm milk. She had always hated the taste of milk and didn't want to submit to that remedy, but on the other hand she didn't want to be up all night because she knew no matter how much sleep she got, Jaheim would be waking her up at 5:00 a.m. and whisking her away to the whore's life.

Sighing in defeat, she stepped out of bed and slipped her bare feet into her house shoes, praying there weren't any roaches within them, or even worse: a mouse or two. Just the thought of that caused her to hug herself and rub her arms.

As soon as she got to the bedroom door, she started to wonder where Jaheim was. He usually slept right beside her. She felt a twinge of jealousy shoot through her as she imagined him laid up with one of the other girls. It seemed like they were growing further and further apart lately, and she wondered if it was because of the baby growing inside of her.

As soon as she got into the hallway, she heard the sound of R. Kelly bellowing throughout the speakers of the small radio. She also heard what sounded like voices.

The apartment was completely dark. She was having a hard time seeing in front of her. Her mind began to play tricks on her, and she got to thinking at any moment a rat could jump out and run up her leg. She started to take huge steps, making her way to the sounds of the music. It led her outside of the second bedroom.

Before trying the knob, she decided to put her ear against the door to see what exactly she could hear. Though the music was on, she could still make out the voices and what was being said clearly.

She heard Amber say, "That's so hot. I love watching you two together. Just seeing how passionate you are drives me nuts."

"Yeah, I know," said her little sister. "Don't you wish that growing up Jeff was like this with us?"

She moaned. "Oh, hell yeah. That would have been awesome."

Tiny felt confused. She wondered what they were talking about. Suddenly she started to feel like she was being left out of a party, and that made her a bit angry. She started to wonder again if everybody there was treating her the way they were because she was pregnant.

She tried the door knob, and to her benefit it was unlocked. Just before she pushed the door in, she started to hear a bunch of moaning and the bedsprings going haywire. Now she knew she had to see what was going on, especially because the woman who was moaning seemed as if she was getting it done to her real good. Before she even looked in and saw what was going on, she found herself getting aroused.

She slowly twisted the knob as to not interrupt the clandestine romp going on inside. Once it was open far enough for her to peek her head in, she did so, and what she saw totally blew her mind back.

There was Amber sitting on the small loveseat in front of the bed with her legs spread wide, and in between them her arm moved back and forth so fast it seemed as if it were a blur. The woman did not take her eyes off of the bed, and in order for Tiny to see what exactly she was looking at she had to open the door farther, which she did. And then her mind was really blown back.

She followed her gaze to the bed and saw Amber's sister laid on her back with her knees to her chest, and a black girl had her head between them, circling her head in huge figure eights while Megan moaned louder and louder as if she were being killed. Tiny couldn't figure out who the black female was until she lifted her head. It was Brandy. She watched as Brandy reached beside her and picked up a huge dildo, sucked on its end, and then began working it into the girl until she had it deep in her. Only then did she proceed to plunge it into her at blazing speeds again and again.

This wasn't what shocked Tiny, though. No, this was only the beginning of her shock. What blew her mind back was what she saw taking place behind Brandy. Behind Brandy Jaheim had her ass spread as wide as the cheeks would go, and he had his face between them, driving her into a frenzy — so much so she left the dildo stuck inside of Megan, turned around, and egged him on.

"Oh my God, Jaheim! Daddy, I'm ready. Fuck that tongue, I'm ready for the real deal. Please give it to me!" she begged, trying to rip his dick out of his boxer shorts.

Tiny stood perplexed outside of the door. She could not believe what she was hearing. The girl was actually begging him to fuck her. She couldn't make sense of what was going on. She felt like she should do something to stop it, but she had no idea what she should do. Not only that, but her legs had taken a life of their own, and they were refusing to move.

"Alright, baby, girl, you deserved daddy's dick, so I'm about to give it to you. You sure this is what you want? Tell me how much you want it.

Brandy had already begun pulling his boxers all the way down and off. She could be heard growling deep within her throat as she wrapped her hand around his penis and kissed the head. Then, all at once, she was sucking him like a porn star, trying to talk along with the muscle on her mouth.

It sounded like she was talking with a mouth full of food. "Daddy I been wanting you to dick me down ever since I saw you fuck my friend when we were little. I been working hard in these streets for you. Now come on, you owe me this."

By this time Jaheim was at full mast. She popped his piece out of her mouth and bent over on the bed. He smacked her real hard on the ass, then grabbed his tool and ran it up and down her sex lips, teasing her.

"Stop teasing me and give me what I deserve!" she screamed, reaching back and putting him inside her.

As soon as he felt her heat, he stabbed forward until his stomach was against her ass. Then he grabbed her hips and proceeded to bang her as if she had pissed him off.

Tiny was so stunned she had grown weak in the knees and dropped to the floor in a state of hysteria. She couldn't believe what they were doing, and to make matters even worse, the two white girls in the room were cheering them on and pleasing themselves to the actions that were taking place. There was so much moaning and groaning and skin-slapping it sounded like a hundred people were in the room instead of just four. Jaheim was holding her head down into the mattress and pulling her ass back into him while she screamed and begged him to do her harder.

Megan and Amber began to feel left out, so they crawled up into the bed and took turns kissing Brandy, and then each other.

It took Tiny fifteen minutes or so to gather herself, at which time they were still going at it. Finally, she jumped to her feet and kicked the door in.

"What the fuck are y'all doing in here?" she screamed, causing the white girls to scatter like roaches, pressing their backs up against the wall.

Jaheim continued to fuck Brandy with all of his might. Tiny could see the veins protruding in his neck, and Brandy had slight tears running down her cheeks. She ran her tongue across her lips and continued to bounce back into him.

Tiny felt the tears running down her cheeks. She was shaking as if it was below zero inside the room and she had forgotten to bring her coat. It was like time had stopped all around her, and the world seemed to be frozen in the moment. The only thing that mattered was the two on the bed and how they were dead set on hurting her.

Amber tried to slowly back out of the room. She knew Tiny had a horrible temper, and she had often watched her go at it with Jaheim, blow-for-blow. Although she had lost more than 90 percent of the battles, it still spooked Amber that she would have enough gall to try to fight a man, and a huge black man at that. She felt if she could just silently sneak past Tiny, she wouldn't have anything to worry about, and she'd be able to leave them to deal with the fireworks that were sure to come.

Megan watched as her sister fearfully crept almost past Tiny. She was no more than a few feet away from her when Tiny spun on her toes and slapped her so hard she flew against the wall, slumping down, knocked out with her head between her naked thighs.

Megan began to cry. She knew if Tiny would do that to her sister, she didn't have a chance in hell, because she barely even knew the girl.

Before Tiny could even look at her, she threw her hands up and began to cop a plea. "Say, Tiny, I swear I have nothing against you. I was just following my sister and doing what felt good. I didn't know things would get this out of hand. I'm willing to do anything to ensure you don't slap the taste out of my mouth like you just did her."

Megan's knees were shaking so bad she could barely stand up. She felt hysterical. She didn't know if she should break out crying or try her luck at breaking past her and out of the door. But then again she remembered they were in the Stateway Projects, which meant she wouldn't get as far as the 12th floor before she would have been raped twice. It was either face Tiny head-on, or the latter. She chose to go through Tiny and beg for sympathy.

Tiny saw the girl drop down onto her knees, and even through her anger she couldn't help but laugh. She looked so pathetic with her pretty blonde hair and her blue contact lenses. I was females like her who made things so hard on black women like herself, she thought. She really wondered what the girl was doing in the projects, running behind some two-bit pimp while her rich family stayed at home and worried themselves sick over her and her sibling. Tiny just felt deep down in her bones the girl had no real reason for being there, she was simply acting out just because it was considered cool, and that disgusted her.

"Bitch, get up. Ain't nobody thinking about you. I don't even know you. I know your sister, that's why I smacked the shit out of her, because she know that trifling-ass nigga is my man, and his sister is like a sister to me. She was supposed to say something instead of joining in and getting off to the shit."

Megan didn't hear a word she said after she'd admitted she wasn't thinking about her. She slowly got to her feet and made her way out of the bedroom door. As soon as she walked past Tiny, she felt her grab her by her long ponytail, and before she knew what was happening her face was being crashed into the wall.

"Sike, bitch! You just as guilty. Now, get your sister and get the fuck out of here!" she screamed as she watched blood pour from the girl's nose.

Megan tried to pick her sister up, but she was knocked out cold. It was like trying to move a dead body. She felt like the task was nearly impossible to do alone, but all it took was for her to look over at the fuming Tiny, and with every ounce of strength in her body she dragged her sister out of that room and closed the door.

Tiny turned to the bed, where the pair were starting to put on their clothes. She felt red hot, and sweat began pouring from her forehead. She silently stared at them for a long time without moving.

Brandy refused to give her any eye contact. She knew what she had done was considered wrong, but it irritated her that night-in and night-out she busted her ass for him just as hard as the other girls, and she was never shown his ultimate affection. The forbidden act itself never bothered her – that just didn't matter. The portion of the ordeal she felt she was wrong about was the dilemma of Jaheim being Tiny's man. She respected Tiny and never wanted to cross her, but everyone knows what they say about curiosity killing the cat.

"Brandy, why you can't look at me, huh? I thought you was supposed to be my little sister. This how you do me?"

Tiny watched as the girl slipped her bra into place over her breasts. She still refused to pick her head up and give her eye contact.

"I'm sorry, Tiny. I don't know what I was thinking. I guess I just let the liquor get the better of me," she said, barely above a whisper.

Tiny stood looking her over with a hand on her hip, trying to decide what she should do next. A part of her wanted to hurt the girl and make her feel as bad as she had made her feel. She started to nod her head up and down, imagining the possibilities. She didn't know what she was going to do yet, but she knew it was going to be good.

Jaheim laid back on the bed with his hands behind his head. He found the whole scene amusing. He felt women were supposed to fight over him, that it was a sign he was putting it down the way he was supposed to. He didn't feel like he owed her an explanation. He felt a pimp was supposed to fuck all his women once they earned his pipe. He didn't care Brandy was his sister. If she went out there and got that cash for him, she could earn the pipe, too.

"Tiny, come here, baby, and let's talk about this."

Tiny scrunched up her face so hard it almost got stuck. "What the fuck you just say to me?"

He reached onto the night table and grabbed a rolled weed-stuffed cigar and lit it. "You heard me. I said bring yo' ass over here so we can talk. I ain't gon' ask you no more, either."

Tiny smiled, a million thoughts running through her mind. "Okay, daddy. Here I come." She walked over until she was standing in front of him.

"You see, that's what I'm talking about. We ain't gotta be up in here fighting. It's enough of me to go around." He pulled her down by the neck and forced his tongue into her mouth.

All Tiny could taste and smell was the essence of Brandy. It started to make her feel sick. Jaheim smelled horrible to her. He smelled as if he hadn't had a shower in a few days, and he'd been having sex every day without washing his behind.

She felt herself gag once, twice, and then she was throwing up into his mouth. It just kept coming. She heard him underneath her, gurgling on the vomit, and out of the corner of her eye she saw Brandy start to puke and purge her guts, and that made her even more sick. By the time she was done, Jaheim was fully coated and hunched over, also regurgitating all he had eaten.

Jaheim could not believe what had just taken place. He was hunched over on all fours coated in only God knows what. He looked over and pointed at Tiny. "Bitch, I'm about to kick yo' ass so muthafucking good for this." He was struggling to control his breathing.

Tiny sat against the wall, feeling like she had contracted the flu. She wondered how a person could allow themselves to smell as bad as he did. Then she wondered how Brandy could be whorish enough to hop on top of him. She felt they both were really sick.

She started to stand up and felt a wave of nausea coming over her, so she began dry heaving.

Jaheim jumped up and grabbed her by her hair.

"Oh, no you don't, bitch. Take yo' ass in that bathroom over the toilet. Then, when you done, you gon' come in here and clean all this shit up. Do I make myself clear?"

She felt so weak all she could do was nod.

***

It was four hours later, and Tiny was finally able to get to sleep after she had cleaned the entire house from top to bottom. She had set out to only clean the room they had their accidents in, but then decided to clean the entire house. She felt it had been long overdue.

She also noticed she was living with three Vikings. They were total pigs who never cleaned up after themselves. They had excessive plates in the sink with food all over them, along with cups that were half filled. There were so many roaches in the sink that as soon as she turned the light on they began scattering like she was Godzilla. All she could do was shake her head and pray for better days.

She had to change the mop water four times because the floor was so nasty, and two times she was chased out of a certain area because rats kept jumping out at her. All in all, the task had worn her out, and the ruffled mattress felt good under her body.

Jaheim walked up to her sleeping form and smacked her with all of his might on her ass. It sounded like a horse being slashed by a jockey. She jumped so fast she fell out of the bed and onto her side on the floor, pulling the sheets down with her.

"Ah! What the fuck is your problem?" she screamed. He had terrified her, and her ass was throbbing.

Jaheim looked down on her with a snarl on his face. "Bitch, where the fuck is them white girls at?" he spat with saliva shooting out of his mouth.

"White girls?" Tiny was confused. She had no idea what he was talking about. She wondered if "white girl" was a code word for something else. "What, are you talking about your cocaine? And if so, I don't know. You know I don't do that shit!"

Jaheim watched her stand up and slowly start to crawl back into the bed. He ripped the sheet off of her, pulling her leg until she fell to the floor again.

She looked up at him like he had lost his mind. She wondered what was going on with him. She got to thinking maybe he was high and just having a bad trip or something, although she wasn't really sure if people actually experienced bad trips off of cocaine.

"I'm not talking about no damn dope, I'm talking about Amber and Megan! Where the fuck are they? I know you done did something, so I'm giving you to the count of three to tell me just what, or I swear on everything I love I'm about to stomp a mud hole in your ass." He pulled his shirt over his head to further drive home his point.

Tiny felt the butterflies in her stomach. "I don't have no idea what you're talking about. I haven't said a word to those girls since yesterday. Why didn't you ask your precious Brandy?"

He pulled his belt out of its loopholes. "Bitch,

this ain't got nothing to do with her." In one motion he slashed it across the air and it collided with her check, causing her to scream out in agony. Before she could digest that blow, he followed with another one. This time it caught her neck and shoulder. She tried to flee away from him, but he pushed her onto her stomach and rained down lash after lash onto her back. He then took her by the hair and slammed her face into the floor, knocking her out cold.

Jaheim punched her again and again, finally letting his frustrations out. She had cost him two top-notch hos. Two top-notch white hos at that, and it was simply something he couldn't accept lying down. He felt their time had run its course anyway. He was tired of her and ready to move on with his life.

He yearned for the champagne lifestyle, and he just knew he would be riding those two white girls all the way there, but then Tiny had to happen.

Every time he thought she was about to wake up, he knocked her back out. He did this until his knuckles were incapable of harming her anymore.

T.J. & Jelissa

Chapter 7

When Tiny woke, she found herself lying on her side with a sticky substance all around her. Her head was throbbing, and the entire room kept spinning around her. Her lips felt as if they were as big as boxing gloves, and she couldn't move without feeling a sharp pain in her ribs.

She draped her right arm around her midsection and tried to sit up, but screamed when pain shot up all through her side. "Please, God, help me. I don't know what is wrong with me, but I know you are strong enough to heal me and save me from evil," she said out loud, praying God heard her. She tried to move again, and this time she almost fainted from the pain. She figured her ribs had to have been broken. It was also then she realized she couldn't open her left eye. It was stuck. She trailed her right hand up to it and felt around. It felt like she had a mask on. The more she trailed her hand over her face, the more scared she became. Her head had swelled up to the size of a pumpkin.

I'm going to kill Jaheim, she thought. *I can't believe he did this to me.*

"What am I sitting in?" she hollered. She reached her hand down and ran it through the liquid substance on the floor. She touched it and ran her fingers together. The fluid was very warm and sticky. She started to panic.

When she came to the realization of what it was, she passed out.

***

This time when she woke up, she was in a hospital bed with so many things in her arms she looked like they were trying to turn her into a robot. She felt weak and highly drained. Her head was still spinning, and her neck felt as if it couldn't hold up the weight of her dome.

She looked to her left and saw Amber sleeping in the chair next to the hospital bed. She tried to call her name and only managed to make small sounds.

Amber heard her murmuring and opened her eyes. "Oh, my God, Tiny, are you alright? You want me to get the nurse?" She jumped up. "Nurse! Nurse, please, we need your help!" she shouted at the top of her lungs.

The nurse ran into the room in a state of panic. She rushed to the side of Tiny's bed and placed her hand onto her forehead, then she looked over to the monitors.

After reading the screens and checking her vitals, she looked over at Amber as if she had lost her mind. "I don't understand, what was the emergency? She seems to be doing fine after losing so much blood."

Amber shrugged her shoulders. "I figured since she had woken up you'd want to speak to her and tell her what's going on. You know, about the other thing." She said this while bucking her eyes.

Tiny was starting to freak out all over again, and the monitors that kept track of her heartbeat told them just that because it began to beep. "What's going on? What other thing are you talking about? Somebody tell me something," she said, trying to sit up in the bed.

"Ma'am, you need to calm down. You're going to be okay, but you have to take it easy. You have lost a whole lot of blood. Your heart is working hard enough, and you don't want it beating as fast as it is right now. That can be very harmful to your health."

Tiny felt like someone was choking her. "My health? What do you mean, my health? Don't you mean my and my child's health?"

As soon as those words left her mouth, she looked over to Amber, and her reaction told her everything. The girl had tears in her eyes. Mascara ran down her cheeks.

"I'm so sorry, Tiny, but you lost it. You lost your child. I'm so sorry!"

All Tiny felt was her head hitting the pillow.

***

When she awoke this time, Amber was just coming out of the bathroom. She had on a whole new set of clothes, and her hair was even different. She pressed the remote on the side of the bed to make it rise. Her mouth felt incredibly dry.

Amber saw she was awake and rushed to her side. "Hey there, my sister, how are you doing?" She placed her hand onto her forehead and then kissed her on the cheek.

Tiny tried to swallow. "My throat is so dry," she said in a raspy voice.

Amber held up one finger, disappeared, and came back two minutes later with a juice box. She popped the straw into the foil part and placed it to Tiny's lips. "There you go, drink up."

Tiny tried to swallow the whole carton in one gulp. She felt like she hadn't had anything to drink in ages. As soon as the liquid hit her throat, she started to feel so much better. She cleared her throat. "How long was I out for?"

Amber ran a cool rag across her forehead. "It's been eight days now. They thought it would be best to keep you under until your vitals stabilized. You've went through some very traumatic things. Every time you came to your brain would snap back to reality, and that would cause your adrenaline to kick in, which increased your heartbeat, and your body was going haywire. They thought this would be the safest way. I'm so sorry you had to go through this. I was so stupid. You were right to kick my ass."

Tiny leaned her head back onto the pillow. "He fucked me over. He killed my child and put me in the hospital. I will never forget this." She sat up slightly on her elbows. "Where is he now?"

Amber shrugged her shoulders, then rubbed her eye. After pulling on her eyelashes, she flicked something and turned back to Tiny. "I don't know. I took my sister back home after she broke down, then I came back to the apartment and found you laid out in a pool of your blood. I had to run all the way back down 13 flights of stairs, call the police, wait until they got there, then bring them back upstairs to where you were, and they helped me carry you back down. The paramedics came, and that's how you got here to Mount Sinai Hospital."

She shook her head. "I think those cops were more afraid of going into the Stateways than I was my first time." She fanned her face with her hand. "I haven't seen or heard from Jaheim ever since you busted up the rendezvous that night. But I did give the cops a description of him, even though we both know they don't care and won't even try to find him."

Tiny agreed by nodding her head. "Yeah, I know, but what are you gonna do, you know?" She gave Amber an incredulous look. "Say, why are you being so nice to me, anyway? I thought you would be the last person to come to my aid."

Amber pulled her purse into her lap, and for a few seconds avoided eye contact with her. "I don't know why you'd think that. I was in the wrong, and I deserved what you did to me. I don't hold any ill feelings toward you because of that. I still feel like you're my sister, and I hope you still look at me as yours."

Tiny felt her heart warm over. If it had not been for the blonde girl, she would have probably been lying inside a freezer in the morgue instead of in a hospital bed on her way to recovery. She had lost the child growing inside of her, and for that one day she promised to make him pay, but she saw no reason to hold a grudge against Amber. After all, she was just doing what the average female who followed a pimp would do.

"Amber, we're cool. Thank you for saving my life. I owe you for that."

Amber shook her head. "No, you don't. I swear we are more than even. I mean, you have still lost so much. I feel horrible right now."

Tiny didn't know what to say to that. Luckily, the nurse came into the room and began to check on her. After she left, Tiny turned to Amber and noted she held her head downward as if something was bothering her.

She cleared her throat. "Amber, what's the matter? Are you okay?"

Amber nodded and gave her a weak smile before frowning and breaking into tears. "No, I'm not okay. I know he is looking for me, and I am so afraid of what he's going to do when he finds me. I just keep picturing you laying in a pool of your own blood. I mean, if he can do that to you, and he's known you since high school, what the hell is he going to do to me?" She slapped her hands over her face and sobbed loudly.

Tiny shook her head and laid back into her pillow. She didn't have an answer for her because she didn't even know what she was going to do when she left the hospital. She felt broken and so lost. Instead of responding to her, she decided to say a silent prayer in her head.

***

"Pastor, I want to thank you so much for allowing us to stay here. I promise you we're going to try and make the stay as short as possible. And are you sure Mrs. Moore is okay with this?" Tiny asked, setting her suitcase on the floor by the bed.

Amber was silent the whole time. She stayed close to Tiny's arm, not wanting her to leave her sight. She felt this would be an opportunity for a new beginning. She was thankful to be taken in. She knew she could not survive on the streets for long without Jaheim tracking her down and possibly ending her life. She also was pregnant and didn't know how to tell Tiny without hurting her feelings or making things become complicated.

"Sister, don't you worry about Mrs. Moore. She is fully aware of everything that is going on, and she gives me and you guys her full support. The Lord said do unto others, and that's just what we're doing. He's blessed us with a beautiful home, and who are we to not share it with the brethren?" He placed the clean blankets on the bed along with the sheets. "Dinner will be in an hour, and I expect both of you young ladies to be washed and there at that time. Do you understand me?"

They nodded their heads in unison and watched as the pastor walked out the door and closed it behind him.

As soon as the door closed, Amber let out a sigh of relief. "Geez, I feel weird being in a holy house. I feel like in any moment I'm going to melt or something." She plopped down on the big bed.

"Girl, you're tripping. Everybody sins. Just because they go to church every Sunday do not make them better than us. They just have the discipline that we lack. Talking about you feel like melting? You know you dramatic for that one," she laughed, opening up her suitcase.

Amber felt a little embarrassed at her comment now. She blushed. "Well, you know what I mean, though." She knelt down and unzipped her suitcase as well. "Look at what all I got in here. I don't know what to wear around these people. All I got is ho clothes."

"Girl, so what? That's all I got, too, but he know what we are, so why should we try to act like we aren't that? All I got is booty shorts for now, so that's what I'm going to wear. Once we get our funds up, then we can buy some clothes, but for now we gotta make do with what we got."

Amber looked at her with one eyebrow raised. "Are you sure?"

Tiny stood up with an outfit in her hands. "I don't know, do you got a better idea?"

***

"Let us bow our heads and give thanks. Lord, we thank you for the food we are about to consume. We pray you bless it and help it to nourish our bodies, and we give honor to you within our minds. Please bless our guests and cleanse them of their iniquities as you also cleanse us. Thank you for your love, and the blood of your son. We pray you continue to hold us within your embrace. We ask these things as well as all things within Jesus' holy and precious name. Amen."

Tiny looked onto her plate at the fried chicken, baked macaroni and cheese, collard greens, and cornbread, and Mrs. Moore had already said for dessert they would be having chocolate-glazed pound cake. She didn't know where she would put all the food, but she was so thankful to have it.

Across the table, Amber's eyes were so big it

looked as if they were getting ready to pop out of her face. She was just a small girl, and Tiny knew she was a very picky eater. She laughed to herself and thought, *That girl gon' definitely put some weight on now.*

Just as they started to eat, the pastor spoke up. "Amber, littler sister, are you alright? You look like you're ready to run out of your chair or something," he said, crumbling his cornbread onto the top of his greens and reaching for the bottle of Louisiana hot sauce and pouring so much onto his chicken and greens it looked as if it was about to pool off of his plate. When he saw that happening, he squirted a little bit more.

Amber snapped up fast in her seat and grabbed her fork. "Yes, sir, I'm fine. I was simply lost in thought. Everything looks good, though. Thank you, Mrs. Moore," she said, picking the skin off of her chicken and setting it to the side as if it were roadkill.

Mrs. Moore smiled. "You're welcome, baby. I hope you enjoy your meal. There is plenty more where that came from, but make sure you leave some room for dessert." She picked up her glass of wine, took a sip, swished it around in her mouth, and then swallowed.

The pastor was smacking so loud it sounded like somebody was jumping rope in his mouth. He took a big bite off of his chicken, at the same time forking up a huge pile of his macaroni and cheese, then he swallowed it all together. "Sister, you know you put your foot in this. Mm, mm! This food so good I'm surprised I ain't found one of your toenails in it." He picked up the huge glass of Kool-Aid, and chugged down the red substance, burped, excused himself, and went back to devouring his meal with both hands.

Tiny stopped mid-chew to watch him. It was like he was putting on a skit all by himself. Even though he was eating like a barbarian, she still found him to be unbelievably attractive for an older man. Even with grease all over his face and his Kool-Aid mustache.

From the other side of the table, Amber could see Mrs. Moore was beyond embarrassed. Her light-skinned face had turned a bright shade of red, and she was refusing to make eye contact with anything other than her plate. They heard the pastor burp again.

"Come on, Harold, don't forget we have guests. You have to mind your manners."

He took the huge napkin off his lap and wiped his face. "Mind my manners? Woman, this food is blessed by the Lord, and I'm gon' enjoy it like He cooked it Himself. This is exactly how I would have been eating at the last supper. Jesus would have said 'Brother Harold, now that's how you eat.'" He laughed to himself, grabbed a drumstick, and took a big bite and chewed it with his mouth open. "Now, if I get to chewing with my mouth open, then that's when you say, 'Pastor, you done lost your manners.'"

Tiny was doing everything she could not to bust out laughing. Here she was thinking the pastor was going to be this straight-laced dude with a religious stick stuck up his you-know-what, but he was turning out to be a normal man. All he wanted to do was enjoy his food in peace. There was no harm in that. Tiny always loved a man who wasn't afraid to enjoy his food. She didn't think he was doing anything wrong.

Tiny was just finishing up their meal when the doorbell rang. Mrs. Moore excused herself from the table, and they could hear her answer the door in her most pleasant voice. A minute later, she walked in with a girl around their age. "Ladies, this is our daughter. Her name is Lisa."

Lisa waved her hand through the air and smiled at them. She leaned down and kissed her father on the cheek. "Hey, daddy, are you enjoying your meal?" She took the napkin and started to wipe his mouth, laughing. "Ladies, you have to excuse my father. When it comes to him enjoying his meals, there is nothing anyone can tell him, so don't try," she warned, wagging a finger at them as if she were scolding.

Tiny looked her up and down and had to admit she was beautiful. Her mother was Asian and black, and it seemed like Lisa had gotten all of her gorgeous features, though she had inherited her body from her father's side of the family, because she was stacked. Tiny felt like a man the way she was ingesting her.

If Tiny was guilty, then so was Amber. There was something about Lisa that gave her a tingle, so much so she had to rub her thighs together.

Lisa turned to Tiny. "I think I remember seeing you in church a few times. Ain't your mother sister Johnson?" she asked, pinching a piece off of her father's cake.

Tiny nodded slowly. "Yeah, that's my mom. I don't think I remember seeing you, though. I definitely wouldn't have forgot if I had." She blushed immediately after hearing herself say that. She scolded herself for flirting with a female, especially a female of a pastor, and in their home. A home they had taken her and her friend into after a traumatic experience. What was she thinking? She lowered her head, and then looked up.

Lisa was smiling down on her. "Hey, how about we do the dishes and get to know each other? Then, later on, maybe us three can watch a movie. You know, kick back and relax. Is that cool with you two?"

Both Tiny and Amber nodded and smiled.

Chapter 8

"I like it here. I wish this was our real life and we didn't have to go back out into those streets in a few weeks," Amber said, wrapping her long hair into one ponytail. "I feel like we're living in some kind of dream, and I really don't want to wake up."

They had just finished doing the dishes together and were waiting for Lisa to come from downstairs so they could all watch a movie to end the night.

"Well, the pastor did say we could stay for as long as we wanted," Tiny chimed in.

Amber turned away from the mirror, then looked over her shoulder and down to her ass, admiring its reflection. "Yeah, but I doubt he meant we could stay forever. Though it is tempting to try." She pulled up her short shorts even higher until the bottoms of her cheeks were showing. Then she ran her hands over them and squeezed. She made eye contact with Tiny in the mirror and blushed. "What are we going to do? What is our plan, or don't we have one?"

Tiny ran her fingers through her weave. It was about time for a new do, and she had no money to pay for it. She was also already starting to get restless from laying around the house and not doing anything. There was also the fact nature was calling. Her body was in need of some good loving. She knew that to be true because everything was starting to arouse her. In that moment she couldn't take her eyes off of the bottom cheeks of Amber. She almost felt drawn to her.

"Well?" Amber whispered.

Tiny walked over to her and put her arms around her and carelessly allowed her hands to plant themselves onto her backside. "Don't worry, I'll figure some things out for us. Let me sleep on it and come at this with a clear head."

Amber nodded. "Okay." She wrapped her arms around Tiny's neck and held her tighter, especially when she felt her running her hands all over her ass. She moaned into her ear when she felt her cup them and squeeze.

There was a loud knocking on the door. Both girls jumped backward and walked away from each other, obviously caught up in the moment. For as long as they had been friends, nothing like that had ever happened. It made them both feel a little guilty. Tiny walked to the door, and before she could ask who it was, it opened and Lisa stepped into the room holding a tape in her hands.

"You girls ready to watch Eddie Murphy play a vampire, or what?"

***

This was Tiny's first time seeing a big screen television up close and in someone's house. What made it even crazier was the fact it was in a girl's bedroom. She wondered just how rich the pastor really was to be able to afford such a luxury for his daughter.

They crawled into her big bed and watched as she popped the movie in. When she bent over to slide the tape into the VCR, her short nightgown rose enough to let them know she had neglected to wear panties. Amber and Tiny snapped their necks and gave each other a knowing look, then laughed silently. She came back to the bed and sat in the middle of them and pulled the big blanket over them.

The room was in utter darkness as they waited for the movie to get past its opening credits. Lisa had popped a huge bowl of popcorn and sprinkled it with seasoning salt. She sat up and with the remote turned the volume up and whispered into Tiny's ear.

"My parents are asleep, and when they are out they are out like a light. Y'all want to smoke a joint or something?"

Tiny thought her ears were playing tricks on her. She had been weeks without the green monster, and there was no secret about it, she was fiending for the sticky. She pressed her ear closer to Lisa's mouth. "Say that again?"

Lisa giggled. "I said I got a little bit of bud. Do y'all want to smoke it with me, or am I going to be doing it by myself?"

Tiny didn't know how Amber heard her over the loud television, but somehow she did. "Girl, count me in. Light that and pass that, please."

Lisa nodded. "That's what I'm talking about. I see you got a little swag in you, white girl."

Amber started laughing. "And I see you got a little devil in you, preacher's daughter."

"Don't we all?"

***

Tiny didn't know where the girl had gotten the

weed from, but she was so high all she could do was smile and listen to the music going off in her head. She felt so good it seemed as if she were in the movie they were watching. She had seen it a million times, but it had never been as good as it was that night.

They were about three quarters into the movie when she felt a hand on her thigh, squeezing. At first it shocked her, causing her to straighten her back and freeze in place. The hand started to rub upward until it landed on her stomach, rubbing in circles. She continued to watch the movie as if nothing was happening. The marijuana was beginning to take effect, because everywhere the hand touched it ignited a fire within her. Then it got bolder and started to descend toward her goodie box. She moaned deeply in her throat and slowly opened her legs, yearning for the caresses to go on. It seemed as if she hadn't been touched in ages. Her body called out for pleasure.

Amber peeked from the corners of her eyes when she heard Tiny moan. Then the blanket moved and her knees could be seen opening. She wondered what was going on under the blanket, though she figured she had a good idea.

Lisa trapped Tiny's left knee between her own legs. This gave her all the access she would need. She felt under her short skirt until she came into contact with her thong underwear. The heat from them seared her hand. It was like a strong magnet drawing her closer until she found herself pulling them to the side.

Amber heard Tiny groan, then she saw her

hump her hips off the bed. Lisa had turned onto her side, and now she could clearly make out her arm moving back and forth at full speed under the blanket. The noises Tiny made excited her. She pulled the blanket over her head to get a better view.

The first thing she saw was Lisa's gown had moved upward and was now stuck along her waist. She was naked from the waist on down. Amber had never seen a booty so big and round, and before she could control herself, she had taken a bite out of it.

This made Lisa suck harder on Tiny's lip. She continued to please her while their tongues wrestled. She felt the white girl behind her spreading her butt cheeks, and then her tongue. She loved the way she was handling her rough back there.

She rose onto her knees ad bent over Tiny's body to give the girl better access to do whatever she wanted. She then took Tiny's legs, threw them on her shoulders, and trapped her face between her thighs.

That night they all did things to each other that made it hard to face the others in the morning at breakfast.

***

"Alright, girl, it been almost two months already. We have to get out of here and get our life on track, because it seem like sister Moore starting to get a little restless with us," Tiny said, biting into her Big Mac.

Amber chewed on her fries and dunked a chicken nugget into the sweet and sour sauce. "I thought only I was picking up that vibe from her. You mean to tell me you was getting that from her, too?"

As of late, Tiny had noticed Mrs. Moore was starting to make a lot of nonchalant comments. She was rolling her eyes at them every chance she got, and she had started a habit of placing the classified ads onto the breakfast table every morning. It was like she was trying to get them to get the hint she wanted them out.

The pastor, on the other hand, seemed as if he was fine with them being there. He would greet them every morning the same way, and he seemed to be taking a special interest in Amber. Tiny saw how he followed the girl around the room with his eyes whenever she was present in her little shorts, which was always.

"Naw, you aren't the only one. I've noticed her looks and comments as well, but I ain't tripping, though. We gon' get out they house soon."

Amber popped the chicken nugget into her mouth just as a fly landed onto her forehead. She swatted it away, but it came back and began to crawl across the table. She tried to smash it, but it flew away and into the back of the restaurant. Amber looked irritated. "But where are we going to go? We don't have no money, and no food."

Tiny nodded. "I know, but we gotta figure something out."

***

That night, Tiny tossed and turned in her bed. She had a tank full of pee that she had to let out. She flipped the covers off of her and stepped onto the floor. She smiled and thought to herself it felt so good not having to worry about roaches or stepping down into something worse.

She bucked open her eyes until they adjusted to the dark room and she was able to see in front of her. Then she started to make her way to the bathroom. The house seemed awfully cool, and she wondered if she should go back and put on her house shoes, because the last thing she needed to be was sick. She knew they would have to get out there and grind within the next few days or so. They could not continue to rely on the shelter of the pastor and his wife. The only thing was Tiny didn't even know where to begin. The last thing she wanted to do was to go back to the life of being a prostitute, but what other alternative did she have? It was all she knew.

The streets of Chicago were rough. They didn't give a fair chance to fully learn them before they were swallowing a person whole and spitting them out in a morgue or a prison. She had lost so many of her peers to the streets. Before she was even in the seventh grade she had already been to thirty funerals, and 20 of them were for children the same age or slightly older than she.

Then there were the ones who had not passed. They were either strung out on some type of narcotic or addicted to the life of selling it. It was like in Chicago a person was either born to be destroyed, or born to destroy. Either way, there was a cycle of destruction, and it was up to each person to choose what side they would be on.

Being successful only crossed her mind when it came to her becoming a famous poet like Maya Angelou. She felt she had so much pain within her that needed to be expressed through the pen. She often wrote her cousin who was incarcerated her poems, and he in turn wrote her his. He had been locked away for three years, and he told her that her poetry got him through – that and the occasional visit.

She felt deep within the pit of her stomach that her written words would pave the way toward her success, she just didn't know where to begin. She figured she'd simply get on her knees before the night was over with and ask God for direction. After all, she was in a Holy house. That had to hold some kind of weight.

She felt like a new woman after she relieved herself. She washed her hands and took a second to look into the mirror. Running her fingers through her hair, she gave a disgusted look.

Her weave was screaming to be replaced. Her face had healed up nicely; there wasn't even a trace of what happened to her. She smiled and put both dimples in her cheeks on display, then cheesed and took a look at her teeth. She ran her tongue over them and zoomed in on the slight gap in the upper row. As a child she had always hated it. The girls made fun of it, and she thought the boys stayed away because of it. But as she got older, she began to notice most men thought her gap was sexy. So she started to embrace it. She trailed her eyes back up to her hair and exhaled loudly.

She heard someone coming down the hallway. She didn't want whoever it was to walk in on her in the bathroom, so she thought that it would be smart to flush the toilet to warn them that someone was in it. They didn't have a lock on the bathroom door, which Tiny found odd. She was ready to flush the bowl when she heard the pastor whispering outside the door.

"Baby, I been fiending for you. Come on, my wife sleep. Let's go in the bathroom."

Tiny's heart began to beat fast. She looked around, not knowing what to do. She didn't want to be caught like a deer in the headlights, but she also was curious to find out who the pastor was talking to. Her curiosity got the better of her, and as the knob on the door began to turn, she dashed into the big tub and pulled the shower curtain around it. The shower curtain for the most part was transparent, but it would have to do. Plus, she didn't mind getting an eyeful. This was just too juicy to pass up.

The door opened and then closed, then Tiny could hear what sounded like a body being thrown up against it. She could hear the sounds of smacking and wet kisses. There was also the feminine moan. It took every ounce of willpower she had to not jump up and see the full picture. Plus, she wanted to know what the pastor was working with in his basement.

"Mm, yes, baby girl. I been thinking about you all day long, just watching you walk around in them little shorts. Did you leave them panties off like daddy told you to?"

More kisses and loud smacking continued to sound throughout the bathroom. "Yes, daddy. You know I do everything you say," Tiny heard Amber say.

She jerked her head back so fast she bumped it. She had to see what was going on. She slowly peeked her head over the rim of the tub and tried to see what they were doing through the curtain.

Amber loved the way the pastor had her pressed up against the door, mauling her breasts as if he couldn't wait to get at them. She had purposely left off her bra to give him easy access. There was something about freaking a preacher while everyone else in the house slept, none the wiser, that drove her crazy. She felt him rip her white beater down the middle and wrap his lips around her left nipple, sucking it hard as if he wanted to pull it off.

Tiny could not believe what she was witnessing. Here was this righteous man, hidden away in the bathroom, defiling her friend in his own house while his wife slept away peacefully in their bedroom. She was shocked, and yet secretly couldn't wait to see how far they would go.

She watched him push Amber's breasts together and take turns slobbering over first one, and then the other. Then he slid his hand down into her shorts. She reached down and unbuttoned them for him.

Tiny felt so aroused and so confused at the same time. She wondered why Amber had not told her about her and the pastor. Why had she decided to keep it a secret? She would definitely question her about it later.

She watched the pastor bend her friend over the sink and rip her shorts down her legs. She kicked them to the side. They crashed against the shower curtain, and Tiny ducked down, fearing they had seen her. She only had a chance to worry about this for a few seconds before she heard the slapping of skin. She peeked over the rim of the tub and her eyes bugged out. There was the Pastor with a hand full of her friend's hair, pulling her head backward while he rammed into her with pure animal lust. He jabbed into her so hard her ass cheeks were turning pink. She scrunched up her face and was literally drooling at the mouth. Tiny had seen her make that face before, and she knew her friend was in ecstasy. She couldn't help being a little jealous. After all, why had he chosen her? Did he think she was prettier than she was or something?

Amber bounced back into him again and again, trying her best to keep up the pace. This man drove her insane. She felt enraptured by the taboo of it all. She needed him, and she felt good to know he needed her as well. She felt everything would fall into place.

The pastor continued to grunt. "Here I come, baby. My sweet, sweet angel. Oh, my baby, here I come!"

Tiny saw him speed up the pace and go full bore into her friend, and then he groaned and Amber opened her mouth so wide Tiny could see clearly down her throat.

***

She watched Amber wash up while the pastor stood to the side of her, admiring her body through the mirror. Amber had already toweled him down with soap, and now she was taking care of herself.

"Daddy, I think your wife is suspecting something, because she's been treating me and Zivial pretty badly. I think it's about time for us to leave here." She bent over and picked up her shorts, her forehead brushing against the shower curtain.

He waited until she stood up and kissed her on the back of the neck. "Don't you worry about her, princess. This is my house, and I pay all of the bills. You let me worry about Mrs. Moore. Don't you let that pretty little mind of yours be concerned, you understand me?" he said, sucking on her ear lobe.

She giggled and pressed back into him. "I love when you sound all defensive of me. That makes me think you actually care and this is about more than, well, you know, sex." She lowered her voice at saying the last part.

"Shush now, baby girl. I already told you that you mean more to me than just that. What kind of a man would that make me if that were true?"

Amber wiggled out of his embrace and turned around to look at him head on. "Come on, now. You know what that would make you. It would make you a man. That's how you all are. You all are looking for an opportunity to take advantage of a female. It been happening to me my whole life." She lowered her head and ran her hands over her face.

The pastor tried to console her by wrapping his

arms around her, but she turned away from him. "Come on, precious, don't be like that. What is it going to take for me to prove to you I am different?"

Tiny's back was beginning to cramp up. She felt like if she didn't get out of that tub soon, she wouldn't be able to. The air was also more stale than she liked. It smelled like sex, and she wondered how they were going to get rid of it before Mrs. Moore got up. Were they even aware?

Amber shrugged her shoulders. "I don't know how you're going to prove it to me, but surely not by words, because I have heard it all before."

He stepped in front of her and grabbed her hands. "Baby, just tell me, what do you need? Please, I'll give you anything."

Amber turned away from him and toward the tub. Tiny could actually see she had a big smile on her face. As soon as it appeared, she snapped it away. She faced him. "Are you really serious that you want to help me?"

The pastor got down onto his knees and laid his head against her stomach. "I'll do anything for you, just say the word. I'll show you I'm different."

Amber looked down on him and kissed his forehead. "Okay, baby. Well, you know we have to leave here soon."

He interrupted, "No, you don't, I already—"

"Listen, Harold, don't cut me off again. I just want you to listen to me, okay?" she said, gripping his chin.

He nodded. "Sorry."

"Now, as I was saying, we have to leave here

soon. That doesn't mean what you and I have has to end, that simply means we can meet other places. Less dangerous places." At saying this, she waved her hand through the air to indicate they were inside the bathroom in his home. This made the pastor lower his head.

"Harold, I want my own place, and I want a nice place, one that I can be comfortable in. I don't want to have to go and work the streets. I don't want to be with any man outside of you. Do you understand that?"

He nodded.

"And I'm going to need some kind of financial help until I can get back onto my feet. I also am not going to allow my best friend to go without, so I want to ensure she's also going to be taken care of."

Tiny smiled and thought it was about time she brought her name up. She had to admit the little white girl had skills she knew nothing about. As she sat back and watched her in action, she started to admire her moxie.

"So, are you going to help me, baby, or were you just saying the things you thought I needed to hear?" She poked out her bottom lip.

The pastor stood up and looked down on her small frame. "I'll take care of everything, don't you worry."

Amber screeched, stood on tippy toes, and wrapped her arms around his neck. "Thank you, daddy. I'm going to be the best little girl you'll ever need." She dropped back down to her knees to show him what she meant.

Chapter 9

"The Bellmont Towers? Are you fucking serious, this is where we will be staying?" Tiny asked with eyes so big it seemed as if her face would get stretch marks.

They were standing in front of one of the most prestigious condominiums in Chicago. Neither girl could contain themselves as they rode up in the elevator. They kept hugging each other and screaming.

"So, when are you going to tell me who the person is that's financing all of this?" Tiny said, though she already knew what was good.

In the weeks that followed the bathroom incident, she had kept her mouth shut and acted as if she was none the wiser. She had hid in the tub on four separate occasions, and two times she had even recorded them together. One thing for sure was Amber had a playbook in her mind that was working. A part of her felt really jealous, but an even bigger part respected her for how she was handling things. So far she had not left Tiny behind, and she had not switched up on her, but Tiny knew the one most important rule of survival was to never be dependent on no one. And as much as she hated to admit it, she found herself totally dependent on Amber.

"Sis, don't worry about all that. All you have to do is lean back and let me twerk this trick. I got us, and I'mma make sure we're always straight, okay." She held out her arms to give Tiny a hug.

Tiny hugged her and held onto her for dear life.

She was thankful for the blonde girl. She thought to herself maybe her intentions were pure.

***

The next morning, Tiny was awakened by Amber jumping on top of her and screaming in her ear again and again. It took every ounce of restraint in her to not beat the hell out of the girl.

"Amber, what the fuck is wrong with you?" she hollered, ready to flip the girl onto her back.

"He bought me a brand new Lexus. It's all pink, just like I asked for. Oh my god, I'm so happy! Get up, sis, we're about to hit the city up in a major way. Come on, I'm taking us shopping," she said, hopping up.

Tiny was still half asleep and a little bit annoyed. She was still trying to process everything Amber had just told her. She could not believe the girl said she was given a brand new Lexus. Those cars had just come out, and they were the hottest thing going in Chicago at the time. The only people who drove them were extremely successful, or so deep in the dope game they were considered King Pins.

She sat up and looked over at her nightstand. The clock read 6:37 a.m.

Amber started to pull the covers off of her. "Get up, sis. We have to get to the mall, then go and get our hair done. And I know you want to go out and eat, so we'll do that, too."

Tiny crossed her arms in front of her. "Girl, I ain't got no damn money to be doing all of that."

Amber smiled and stood over her. "Wait for it – *bam!*" she said, pulling a yellow card out of her bra. "You don't have to worry about anything. It's all on me. Or should I say, we're putting it all on this."

Tiny was dumbfounded. She had no idea what it was the girl was holding in her hands. She was born and raised in the projects, and credit cards didn't exist there. Nobody in the building was given credit for anything. She gave Amber a look that said she had no idea what she was holding.

"What? Oh my god, you're telling me you have never seen a credit card before?" she giggled. "That's funny."

Tiny felt a little bit insulted. "So? That doesn't make you better than me." She scrunched up her face and fluffed her pillow, preparing to lie back down on it.

Amber slid into the bed next to her and wrapped her arm around her shoulder. "No, sis, hey. Look, I wasn't making fun of you. I'm sorry, okay?" She kissed her cheek. "But this bad boy is called a Visa, and with it we can buy anything we want with no questions asked. It has my name on it, so all I will have to do is show them I.D. and sign my receipts. We can get anything you want today. That sound cool?"

Tiny smiled. "Hell yeah, that sounds good. Let's do it."

***

By the time they left the mall, they had so many bags it looked as if they had gone grocery shopping after getting their food stamps. They piled them into the car, laughing at the top of their lungs.

Tiny had bought so many designer outfits she couldn't wait to be seen in. She felt like a kid who had been spoiled rotten, though a huge part of her felt uncomfortable because even though she had all of those material possessions, she did not have any money in her pockets, so anything she needed she had to ask Amber for as if she were her mother.

Amber handed her a cellphone. "Oh, this is also yours, and here is your new number. I paid up the bill for six months, so you're good until then."

Tiny took it and felt her heart skip a beat. "Oh my god, why are you being so nice to me?"

"Wait, what?"

"You heard me," Tiny said, now with tears running down her cheeks. She didn't understand how Amber could be keeping it so real with her. They had never been that cool, and before the hospital incident they would go weeks at a time without saying a paragraph to each other. Now here she was, spending thousands and thousands of dollars on her and buying her a cellphone. She felt in the pit of her stomach something was up, she just didn't have the slightest idea what it could be. Then she started to wonder if maybe this girl was feeling guilty because she was milking a pastor of the church, but quickly washed that out of her mind because she had seen them in action on a few occasions, and there was definitely not any feeling of guilt there. At least, it didn't look that way.

Amber put the car in drive, pulling away from the mall. "I don't know what you're talking about.

What, am I doing something wrong?"

Tiny shook her head. "No, it's just my whole life no one has ever given me anything for free. I have had to bust my ass for it or lay on my back, and here you are doing all of this. What gives?"

Amber frowned. "Nothing gives. I thought we were suppose to be sisters. This is how I would treat my sister. I'm up right now, and you're supposed to be, too. I mean, you didn't leave me on the streets when those religious folk too you in, right?"

Tiny nodded. "Yeah, I guess you're right about that. I'm sorry, maybe I am overreacting to your kindness. I just never had this done before, so you have to excuse me. I am grateful, though." She leaned over and kissed her on the cheek.

Amber smiled. "Thank you. Your kisses make me feel so strong for some reason." She lowered her sun visor. "So, you ready to get that weave redid?"

"Hell yeah."

* * *

Tiny thought she was tripping. Her mind had to be playing tricks on her. She sped up her pace and refused to look over her shoulder. Her stomach was already doing somersaults.

The sun was just starting to go down, bringing on the night. A cool breeze coasted through the city of Chicago. Looking up, she noted it was a full moon. She heard the footsteps behind her again, then the chills shot up her spine. It had to be him, she thought.

The two grocery bags she carried were starting

to feel as if they weighed a hundred pounds apiece. Back at the condo the refrigerator was damn hear empty. They had shopped at every store in Chicago, it seemed, with the exception of one that sold food.

A can skipped across the ground behind her, and the noise nearly made her trip over her own foot. She looked up at the sign that read Lake Shore Drive and knew she only had two more blocks to travel before she made it home safely.

She had visions of breaking out into a full sprint. She would drop the bags and make a run for it if the person behind her was who she thought it was.

She was halfway there when he called out her name.

"Tiny. Tiny! Bitch, I know you hear me calling you," he hissed.

As soon as she heard his voice, she dropped the bags and took off in a sprint for dear life. All she could imagine was him killing her, him beating her senseless until she no longer had the urge to breathe. So she ran and ran until the Towers appeared in front of her. She was no more than 20 yards away from the entrance to the door when she looked back over her shoulder to check how far behind he was, but she saw nothing other than an empty street. This caused her to pause in her tracks.

The air began to become overtly foggy, so much so she couldn't see in front of her. She looked for the entrance to the door, but it seemed to disappear all together. Then she heard the flapping of large wings, and there before her Jaheim appeared in an all-black, tailor-made tuxedo.

"How dare you think you can escape me, Tiny? Don't you know you belong to me? That my blood flows through your veins and without me you are worthy of nothing but death?"

Tiny screamed at the top of her lungs, praying the security guard inside their building would hear her. "Leave me alone, Jaheim! Why won't you just leave me alone?" She took off in a sprint again, but there he was 20 yards ahead of her, staring as if he had a trick up his sleeve.

She felt so confused. She didn't know how one second he could be behind her, and then the next he could be 20 yards ahead.

He slowly walked toward her with his arms held outward. "You cannot run from what is meant to be. You are mine for the taking. And take you I must."

Tiny's head nearly popped off her shoulders when she saw him open his mouth and bright white fangs appeared. Before she could stop him, he jumped onto her and bit into her neck, sucking the blood directly from her body. All she could do was scream.

***

When she came to, Amber was sitting over her with a cold towel placed onto her forehead. Tiny looked into her face and jumped backward. "Oh my god, where is he? He's here, isn't he?"

Amber stood up and looked around nervously. "Tiny, what the hell are you talking about? Who's here?" she asked, starting to freak out.

Tiny raced her eyes around the room. "You

know who I'm talking about. Jaheim! And that fool done turned into a vampire now, he got fangs and everything."

Amber lowered her head. "Shit, girl, you're still tripping off of that Angel Dust. I told you it takes a few days to wear off after your first time."

"What are you talking about?"

"Sis, you're just tripping, and you have been for the last two day. That Mexican dude on the west side where we bought our weed from laced our shit, and that's what has you fucked up right now."

Tiny shook her head from side to side, trying to get rid of the cobwebs. She couldn't remember ever taking any Angel Dust. She also didn't remember them buying weed from the west side. She already knew better than that. She sat on the bed and tried to regain her composure. She had never done any drug in her life, with the exception of marijuana. Now Amber had allowed somebody to take advantage of them, giving them drugs that had her imagining she was being chased by vampires that had taken over Jaheim's body. Not only that, but she continued to feel tremors shoot through her. She felt like she was seconds away from losing her mind. A sudden wave of dizziness came over her, and she fell backward.

Amber rushed to her side, applying the cloth to her forehead that was sweating profusely. Tiny's body was starting to shake uncontrollably. Amber didn't know what to do. She was seconds away from dialing 911 when suddenly Tiny stopped shaking and sat up. She looked around the room, and then ran off into the bathroom.

As soon as she saw the toilet, everything that

was inside of her came out. She purged her guts so hard she thought her insides were turning inside out. Tears sailed down her cheeks, and she had visions of dying. She felt like she was at the end of her life's rope.

Amber rushed in and held her micro braids out of the way so they wouldn't drop into the toilet. She felt horrible for her friend, and she knew she could not tell her it wasn't an accident. She had purchased the drug on purpose with the hopes they could enjoy it together as a change of pace.

Tiny stopped thinking she was about to die and started to pray she would drop dead and get it over with. The pains that shot up through her stomach every time her body tried to force her to throw up were unbearable. She was ready to throw the towel in.

When she started dry heaving for a full minute, she knew she didn't have any more to give. She slipped to the floor.

Amber felt so guilty. "Are you okay, babe? I'm so sorry he tricked us like that. We should have somebody go over there and kick his ass." She wet the towel in the sink and wiped Tiny's face with it.

"Yeah, we should. I feel a little better now, though," she said through a voice so raspy it sounded like she was dying of thirst.

T.J. & Jelissa

Chapter 10

They had been staying in the condo for two months, and things were going well. The rent was paid up always 2 months in advance, and they never had to worry about groceries. They had both gone out and gotten onto public assistance, and an older lady down at the offices had even shown them how to sign up for Section Either, also known as rent assistance. They filled out the paperwork and were told they would be placed onto a waiting list.

Tiny had also been filling out job applications all over town. She thought it was time for her to become a mature woman. She knew she could not depend on Amber forever, even though the girl didn't seem to have any problems with her doing so.

As she came out of the four-star restaurant where she'd just had an interview, she picked up her cellphone and called for a cab. Even though she didn't have any money in her pocket, she knew Amber did, and she would pay for it once she got there.

In a way, it felt good to have everything handed to her, and she wondered how a rich housewife could ever get bored of living that type of lifestyle. It was something she fantasized about every day. She had even had the audacity to pray for it. For that she didn't feel bad, because she was sure she had read somewhere in the Bible that God already knew what you wanted before you even asked, so He already knew.

***

The cab pulled up 15 minutes later, and she got in and immediately cracked a window. The Jamaican man was so musty she couldn't even smell the fish he was eating; all she could smell was his underarms, and he had the nerve to have his shirt off. He was so fat his belly button hole looked like a dark tunnel.

He looked back at her and asked for the address. She gave it to him, and he smiled a yellow, snaggletooth grin that disgusted her to the core.

"Ya 'uh, a gurl as pretty as you shodn't be all alone in dee streetz. Ma glad ya called ma' car, o' else ain't ne telling ware ya might 'ave wond up, ya know?"

She smiled weakly. His breath smelled like the juice at the bottom of a dumpster. She watched him dig in his nose and roll it around between his index finger and thumb before popping it out the window. Then he went back in for the second go around. She felt her stomach turn and prayed she wouldn't throw up. If she had to stay in there longer than five minutes, she knew it was going to happen.

"Hey, you know we'll get there faster if you jump on the expressway," she offered.

"You inna rus little gurl? Ma taught ya won ta talc to ma a liddle bit," he cheesed.

She noted he had a huge booger stuck in his mustache, and there was food all over his mouth. They were at a red light, and he had turned all the way around just to tell her that. Though she tried to resist it, she could not stop dry heaving.

"Ya okay, babe gurl? Ma pull over and giv ya

mouff to mouff, ya?"

She waved her hand through the air and begged him not to. "No, I'm good. I was just burping. I'll be okay."

He smiled and turned around, wiggling his finger in his ear, taking it out, and then looking at it. His eyes got so big, as if he had shocked himself. He popped his finger out the window and kept looking to see if the wax was dislodged. Finally he wiped it on the side of the car.

Tiny thought she would scream when he entered the expressway and there was a huge traffic jam. She sat up and looked out of the front window, and saw the cars were piled up for miles and miles.

Why do I always have the worst fucking luck, she thought. *This type of shit only happens to people like me. Fuck, I don't know how much longer I can survive in this car with this nasty-ass dude.*

He turned around in his seat and smiled. "So, wat's yur name?"

She shook her head and slowly pinched her nose closed. "My name Latrice, and I'm engaged to be married. I have four kids and a dog."

He laughed. "Oh ya? Well ma tink ya man iz crazy fer leeving ya out in the night time. Maybe ya leeve him fer a reel mans like ma." He leaned over the seat and got so close to her face she could see the food still stuck in his teeth. When she heard him fart on the other side, she got ready to punch him in the face. And what made things so bad was the fact the traffic line was not moving.

"Ma sorree. Lactoast intolerable, ya know."

That had taken the cake. "Look, you stanking-ass muthafuck, how you think you gon' run a business and you smelling all foul and shit. You stank so bad you had that window open the whole time, and ain't not one mosquito attempted to come in it. You got food all in your teeth. Are you afraid of a toothbrush or something? And deodorant? Yo ass need some deodorant. You smell foul, dude. If you were my son and you left the house smelling like that, when you got home I'd kick your ass."

She shook her head. "If you were my husband, you'd come home to an empty house. Then, when you fell asleep, I'd wake you up with me and two other people kicking your ass for smelling like that. I'm appalled." She raised her eyebrow and waited for him to respond.

He looked at her for a long time, and then his face started to break up, and he broke into tears. "I hav a condishun. Itz not ma fault," he whimpered, crying real tears. His mouth was open so wide Tiny could see his tonsils moving as he screamed at the top of his lungs.

That completely caught her off guard. Here was this man of 300-plus pounds sobbing like a two year old. She even felt a little bad. But he did stank, and somebody had to tell him. She could not believe nobody had told him that. That blew her mind.

"Git out! Git out rite now, ya stukk-up bitch! Now!" He threw open the door and even upped a pistol on her.

"Hey, now, buddy, calm down. You can't put me out on the expressway. That's unethical," she said, looking around at the traffic that was still frozen.

He cocked back the hammer and lowered his eyes into slits.

She threw open the door in haste and stepped out into the night. The EL train was just going past on its tracks, screaming its departure. Cars all around her were bumping their music and blowing their horns in a pointless attempt to get the traffic flowing. She looked up a few miles ahead and saw the flashing lights of the paramedics and police cars.

How the hell do I get off of this damn highway? she thought. This was pure suicide. She looked over to the cab driver who still sat behind the wheel, crying his eyes out. She had no sympathy for him now. She hoped she had hurt his feelings. What type of man would put a woman out in the middle of the freaking highway just because she told him the truth?

She was making her way to the side of the road when she got in front of a marble-black and red BMW, and the driver rolled the window down and called out to her.

"Say, li'l momma. What, you got a death wish or something? Why you out here walking between these cars like don't nobody love you?" the dark-skinned man said, smiling a mouth full of gold.

She thought he was cute. His skin was so black it accentuated his features. He had the sexiest of lips, nice and full, and his dreadlocks were just the right length. She began imagining the possibilities.

She could hear the 2Pac bumping out of his speakers. Being in Chicago, every girl wanted a thug. It felt like it was impossible to survive out there without one. By the looks of his car and the jewelry in his mouth, he was definitely worthy of her time.

She did her best rendition of looking sad and alone. "No, I don't have a death wish. That crazy cab driver over there just threw me out of his cab because I didn't relent to his advances. Now I'm trying my best to get off of this expressway before the traffic get moving."

She saw him looking her up and down, appraising her beauty.

"And then what? You about to walk all the way home?" He swatted at a moth that was trying to fly into his open window.

Tiny looked around and shrugged her shoulders. "I don't know, I haven't thought that far yet."

The last thing she wanted to do was walk all the way home. There was a 100 percent chance she would not make it. If the rapists didn't get her, some type of female gang would. If they didn't, then maybe it would be a stray bullet, or a wandering dog. The possibilities were limitless.

"I'll tell you what, li'l momma, why don't you get on and I'll drop you off at home. A pretty woman as yourself shouldn't be out wandering the streets. You're an easy target. You're small and all fine and shit." He smiled.

Tiny gave him a hard stare, then popped her hand onto her hip. "How do I know you aren't a crazy maniac that look forward to women jumping out of cabs on expressways just so you can invite them to your car, where you ravish them before throwing their bodies into the river, huh? How can you prove that isn't your profile?"

The cars were starting to move around them. She got nervous and thought to herself maybe she was passing up her only hope of transportation. She didn't want to be stranded all the way on the east side. Rumor had it a huge war was going on over new heroin turf. The last thing she needed was to be caught in the middle of that firestorm.

"Look, shorty, you don't know that. But I can swear to you that ain't my character. My only concern is getting you home, and on the way there getting your phone number, 'cause I can definitely see myself spoiling somebody like you."

That was all she needed to hear. She smiled and walked across to the car as horns sounded all around them. He opened the passenger door, and she slid into the soft leather seats and closed the door. The cool air from the vent blew into her face right away, making her feel a whole lot better after stepping out of the humid night.

"You gotta put your seatbelt on, too, 'cause the Vice been pulling niggas over for that and searching they whole car. That's the last thing I need right now," he said, eyeing her seriously.

Tiny reached and clicked the seatbelt across her chest. "Do you have something in here I should be worried about?"

"Hell yeah."

***

They rode in silence for a little while when he reached over and turned the radio up. 2Pac spit from the speakers, and he nodded his head to the *Me Against the World* album. His car smelled as if he'd just bought it. The bass vibrated every fiber of her being.

She waved her hand through the air, and he reached and turned the system down. He gave her a puzzled look. She flipped her hair off of her shoulders and gave him her winningest smile. "We've been rolling for ten minutes and you haven't even asked me where I lived yet. Don't you think that's important?"

He leaned back in his seat and continued to coast through the night. "Well, I figured I'd at least take you to get something to eat first, get to know you a li'l bit, and then you'd feel more comfortable telling me where you stay. Besides, I kind of like being in your presence."

She looked him up and down, then sat back in her seat, flattered. He was either serious or simply had a way with words. Either way, she was digging him, and up close he was even more handsome. If there was such a thing as love at first sight, this was her first sighting of it.

"Can you at least tell me your name?" she asked.

"Aw, that's my bad. My name Avery. I'm named after my old man, so I guess that makes me a junior."

"So, which do you prefer I call you: either Avery or Junior?"

He laughed and pulled a cigar out of the ashtray. "Call me Avery. Ain't nothing junior about me. If you stick around long enough, you gon' find that out. By the way, what's your name?"

She shuffled uncomfortably in her seat. She had thoughts on making one up, but decided he had kept things real, so she would also. There was no way Avery was a made up name. At least she hoped it wasn't. "My real name is Zivial, but everybody calls me Tiny because of my stature."

He nodded and made a strong right onto a busy street. "So, Tiny, tell me how many kids you got?"

She was taken aback. "What? Why do you assume I got kids?"

He sucked his teeth. "Girl, this is the mid-90's. Everybody got kids, and as fine as you is, I know every nigga that get on top of you be trying to leave one in you. So keep shit one hunnit, how many do you got?"

She frowned. She didn't know whether to be insulted or to take it as him feeling her out. Either way, the question had caught her off guard, and it made her feel a little edgy. "Well, for your information, I don't have any kids. I've only been with one man, and I wasn't ready for kids. My parents are very religious, and I am only a teenager. They would have killed me, and then prayed to God I went to Heaven just so Jesus could kill me again. I would appreciate it if you didn't stereotype me with statistics."

He wiped his hand over his mouth. She couldn't take her eyes off of his thick lips. They were so juicy, she had visions of sucking on them, or watching him pull on her nipples with them. She had no idea what made her make up the elaborate story, but she simply rolled with it. She figured in order to land a man like him, she would have to step outside of the norm. She figured he was used to picking up the average ghetto hoodrat. She thanked the heavens she had recently left an interview and was dressed rather conservatively. Maybe that's where she had gotten the confidence from to relay such a false rendition of her life.

"My bad, Tiny. I didn't mean to come at you like that, but I'm from the Robert Taylor Projects, and every girl over there be having three kids by the time they 17. So, I'm just speaking on what I'm used to."

"It's cool. I ain't meant to react like that. I apologize, and I do thank you for picking me up. I think it's quite gentlemanly of you." She didn't know what the hell she was saying. What was going on in her brain? Maybe it was the angel dust coming back to haunt her again. She had to stop the behavior before she painted a picture of herself that she couldn't live up to.

"Quite what? Man, shorty, you sounding real uppity right now. Don't tell me you from way out somewhere where only white people stay. You is a li'l yellow, which mean you could be mixed and shit."

Tiny started laughing. "Boy, nall. Well, yeah, I do stay around white people now, but I was raised in the Stateway Projects. I been trying to get my life together, though."

He pushed in the car lighter. "You don't mind if I smoke, do you?"

She shook her head. "Of course not, and this is your car."

"It don't have nothing to do with that. It's all about respect. If you wasn't down with me smoking this weed in your presence, I would wait until I dropped you off."

She was beginning to like him more and more. She had never met a man who spoke about respecting a woman. Maybe they were raised different from project to project. One thing was for sure: she didn't want to run him away.

He puffed on the blunt and inhaled a thick cloud. "So, you say you from the Stateways?" His voice was cracked from the weed, and it sounded like he was about to choke. To her surprise, he held his composure quite well. He followed the first toke by four others. "I can't drop you off over there because I got plenty enemies throughout that whole hood. This car'd be swiss-cheesed."

Tiny repositioned herself in the leather seat. "I said I was raised over there. I don't live there no more, and is you gon' let me hit that green or what?" It smelled so good, and she could tell it wasn't the average bag. This was the good stuff people paid top dollar for.

"Aw, my bad, shorty. You should have said something. Here you go." He passed her the blunt, and she liked the fact it wasn't all wet up. Even though he had those big, sexy lips, he knew how to control them. That gave her a tingle. She squeezed her thighs together inside the black Versace skirt.

She took two strong pulls and damn near coughed up a lung. He had to pat her on the back and reach under his seat to give her some of the juice he had been saving. She usually didn't drink behind anyone, especially not a stranger, but her chest felt like she swallowed a gallon of lava. It was either drink the juice or continue on in pain. It was a no-brainer. She took gulp after gulp while he rubbed her back.

"You're ok, sweetheart. I got you."

***

By the time they pulled up in front of her building, she had fallen for him. She was so high she had to lay her head on his shoulder the whole drive. He took her to the Home Run Inn where they ordered two large pizzas to go, and he paid for them without even flinching. He pulled out a knot so big it looked as if he was trying to ball up a dictionary. She was definitely impressed.

"So, I'm gon' see you again, Zivial?" he asked as she opened her door, preparing to get out.

She saw the longing in his eyes, and that again flattered her. She wanted to throw the pizza on the curb, rip his clothes off, and take him in the back seat and ride him reverse cowgirl style. She had visions of rubbing her muffin all over those thick lips while he pulled on them gently and sucked on her vagina's nipple.

Her imagination was getting the better of her and she started to become aroused. She felt her nipples peeking through her blouse and hoped he didn't see them.

She picked up the pizza box to block them. "Yeah, well, I gave you my cell phone number, and you see where I live. I got your pager number, too, so if it's meant for us to see each other again, I'm pretty sure we'll make a way."

He nodded. "Well, alright then. I guess I'll see you later. You take care of yourself, though, and don't be getting stranded no more. You got my number now, so if you need anything, you make sure you hit me up, and I'll be there for you."

She smiled. "Okay, I'll hold you to that. See you later."

"I hope so," was the last thing she heard before he peeled away from the curb with Aaliyah playing in the background.

***

It felt like it took her forever to make it to the elevator. All she wanted to do was to get inside their apartment, take a hot shower, eat a few slices of the pizza, and hit the sack. She was so tired every step felt like two.

The elevator door was on its way to closing when an old white lady hollered for her to hold it. She stuck her hand in between the closers and waited for the woman to make it in there. She was using a walker and moving so slowly Tiny was sure she could have taken the lift up to her apartment and sent it back down to the lobby and the old woman still would have not made it inside yet.

It took her a full five minutes to get there, and by that time Tiny was so irritated she felt like pushing her down. She didn't even say thank you, simply got on and pressed the floor to her apartment and squeezed herself so far in the corner as if she didn't want to touch her.

Tiny rolled her eyes. "You're welcome, ma'am."

The old lady had the shakes. Her neck bobbed up and down on her shoulders so much it was like it was floating in the air. "For what? That's your job, to hold the door for us, little girl."

"Excuse you?" She just knew she hadn't heard her correctly. There had to be some sort of signal crossing.

"You heard me, little girl. You do work here, don't you? Whose slave are you?" she spat, giving her a look of disgust. Then she started talking to herself out loud. "It was so much easier when we were beating the hell out of the niggers. They obeyed and they paid attention. Now they expect you to say thank you just for them doing their job. This ain't Africa!"

Tiny was so glad the old woman's floor came up and she exited the elevator, because she was seconds away from kicking her ass. The woman must have thought they were still in the 1800s.

Chapter 11

She turned her key in the lock, exhausted. The pizza was still nice and hot, and she could feel the heat on the bottom of the box. She hoped Amber was hungry, and if she wasn't she could always save it for the morning. One thing white people had figured out was cold pizza. It did taste good.

She came in and dropped her key into the cookie jar, sat the pizza on the counter and stepped out of her heels. Her toes were screaming bloody murder. She couldn't wait to soak them. She had unbuttoned her blouse and was about to take it all the way off when the sight in the living room froze her in her tracks.

She thought about running, escaping back out the door, but it was too late. She had already been spotted. Her stomach dropped to her feet. She could not believe what she was witnessing.

She walked further into the living room. "What the fuck is this?" she screamed.

Amber picked her head up from the table after having snorted a healthy line. She was dressed in a long t-shirt, and beside her Jaheim sat smiling up at her. He was shirtless, and Amber was clearly the reason why. Tiny felt so sick to the stomach with anger.

"Amber, what the fuck is going on? What is he doing here?" she screamed at the top of her lungs.

"What is going on out here?" Brandy asked, stepping out of Amber's bedroom in just her bra and panties. She looked as high as a kite.

"Holy shit! Tiny, listen, I can explain. I ran into

them at the mall, and I just wanted to see Brandy, but then I saw him and these old feelings came back, and I'm so sorry. I —"

Before Tiny could even think about what she was doing, she ran at her in full speed, ready to beat her senseless. Jaheim stood up, blocking her path. His face pulled into a snarl. He had lost a few pounds, but he was still a big man.

"Tiny, if you put your hands on her, I'm gon' have to kill you, because she got my baby growing inside of her, and I have to protect its wellbeing."

Tiny shot daggers at Amber. "Bitch, you let this nigga get you pregnant? Are you fucking serious?"

Jaheim looked from Amber, who held her head down, back over to Tiny. "Aw, what, she didn't tell you? She four months. She been pregnant, and we been fucking. You ain't gotta worry about nothing, though, 'cause bitch, I'm through with you. You're dismissed. You and I have no more business. It's all about me and Amber."

"And me!" Brandy chimed in, not wanting to be left out.

She plopped down on the couch beside Amber and held her hand. Jaheim did not take his eyes off of Tiny. There was an eerie silence in the room. He gave her a look of hatred. She returned his glance with the same emotion. She refused to back down. She was no longer afraid of him. He had taken more from her than he could ever again.

A part of her felt like he had beat the baby out of her purposely. He had to have known what he was doing, and as much as she could recall, she remembered he directed a lot of blows toward her stomach. Now he stood over Amber protectively. That hurt her to the very core.

She wondered why she hadn't noticed the girl being pregnant. She regretted not paying more attention. But then again, she was so damn skinny anyway, so it would have been hard to tell. Still, she felt betrayed. How could she keep such valuable information from her? How could she allow their abuser into their home?

Amber stood up. "You guys, can you go into the room and give me and Tiny a chance to talk, please?"

Jaheim curled up his lips and gave Tiny a look that said he wanted to kill her. He looked her up and down and then reached for Brandy's hand. "Yeah, I guess we can do that. Come on, baby, let's give them a little space."

Brandy followed behind, and together they entered the room and he slammed the door, causing her and Amber to jump.

As soon as the door closed Tiny turned to her. "Amber, what the fuck is going on? How could you do me like this?" She felt the tears welling up in her eyes.

"I don't know. I wanted to tell you, I just didn't know how. I was pregnant at the same time you were, and I knew he was the father. I didn't know how to come out and tell you about any of it because of what you were going through. I'm so sorry, and I swear I never meant to hurt you. But what do you want me to do. Don't my child deserve to have a father?"

Tiny laughed and tilted her head toward the

ceiling. "You gotta be kidding me, right? You actually think that deadbeat-ass dude is going to be there for you and your child? Girl, you'll be lucky if he don't beat it out of you. Do you have any idea what you're getting yourself into?"

She wrapped her arms around her body as the tears sailed down her face. Her nose started to run, causing her to snivel. "I don't know. He's never put his hands on me this far. Why would he start to do it after we had our kid together?"

That revelation cut Tiny so deep that she wanted to break out into tears. Jaheim had been whooping her ass for as long as she had known him. He had never hesitated to beat her. Now here was Amber saying the complete opposite. "Are you saying that for as long as you knew him, he's never hit you?"

The girl nodded. "No, he never has."

Tiny blinked tears. "Well, maybe you two belong together, and that's all I have to say about that." She walked past her on the way to her room and paused. "Oh, and are they going to be staying here for a little while?"

Amber shrugged her shoulders. "I don't know, maybe for a few weeks."

"Okay, that's cool, I guess." She walked away with a smile on her face.

***

It took Tiny three weeks of living with the trio to develop a plan of action. She felt that it was in her best interest to avoid Jaheim as much as she possibly could, and withdraw into herself, in order to properly execute her plan to leave for good. She could not go on staying with them for too much longer without flat-out killing all three. So many nights she would lay in her bed and listen to the sounds of their three-way sex session. All of the grunting and swearing was starting to drive her crazy.

All three walked around the condo in the nude, and at any given time she could catch one duo or the other screwing right there on the kitchen table. It was no holds barred.

They were also extremely filthy. They never cleaned after themselves, and sometimes they went a day or two without bathing. Their apartment was beginning to take on the stench of a homeless shelter.

Jaheim had both girls heavily dependent on drugs. They snorted as much powder up their nose as they did oxygen. What really broke the camel's back was when she came home and found Jaheim with a wire wrapped around his arm and a syringe in his veins, passed out on the couch. It was in that moment she knew she had to get out of there. She didn't even check to see if he was still alive, and hoped he wasn't.

***

She sat in the front of the church and listened to the pastor as he gave his speech. The whole time she felt as if he were lying directly to her. After all, he was speaking about adultery. She felt he was the biggest hypocrite she had ever known.

Afterward, as the church was letting out, she walked over to him and whispered that she needed to speak with him alone, and it was urgent. He gave her a look of concern and nodded. He told her he would meet her in his office in fifteen minutes.

She followed the routine of hugging all of the members of the church that stuck around for those affections. She wondered to herself how many of them were perverts, and how many were genuine believers in Jesus. How could the church be holy when the one leading it was not?

She watched as the members came up one-by-one and dropped their tithes into the collection plates the ushers held at the front of the church. It was customary for one to put in 10 percent of their earnings, and their church was huge. It had a member base of at least 200, and that wasn't counting the stragglers like herself. There was no question the pastor was clocking in off of his flock.

The last few people were heading out the door. She looked across the room and he nodded at her to follow him, which she did. They took the stairs downward, took a left at the hallway, and stopped when they were in front of his office door. He held up one finger as he opened it. As soon as he did, Tiny saw Mrs. Moore sitting at his desk on the phone. She was just hanging it up when they stepped inside.

"That was a powerful sermon today, baby. You did a good job," she said, kissing him on the lips. She looked past him and saw Tiny and gave her a weak smile. "Hello, Zivial. What brings you here today?" she said with a hint of sarcasm. To emphasize her disrespect, she rolled her eyes.

Tiny decided to let her have this moment. She promised herself she would take the air out of her sails at another time. "Hello, Mrs. Moore. I came out to enjoy the pastor's sermon as well, sometimes you just need to be lifted by the spirit. What better way to take flight than by the engines of the pastor and his wonderful sermons?"

The pastor placed his arm over her shoulder. "Aw, little sister, you are too kind. Let us not forget I only speak what I am blessed to. Give all the praises to Him, because His messages is the truth. I am only a shepherd, a vessel." He looked toward his wife. "Baby, would you mind giving us a few moments alone. The sister has some things on her mind that are of great importance."

She looked at Tiny and raised her eyebrow. "I guess I'll go upstairs and count over the tithes with the treasurer of the church. It was nice seeing you again, Zivial. Tell your mother I said hi when you see her, okay?" she said, walking out of the office and closing the door.

The pastor walked over and locked it. He then sat down behind his desk and motioned for her to have a seat. "Would you like anything to drink?" he asked, opening the small refrigerator to the side of his desk.

"Sure, what do you have?" she said, looking down and trying to get a good view inside of the small appliance.

He rifled around for a moment and eventually came out with a Snapple. She accepted it. He placed one on his desk before him as well.

"So tell me, little sister, what is it I can do for you?" He popped the top and turned the drink up, swallowing as if he were dying of thirst.

"Well, sir, I have to be honest. I didn't come in here today to talk about me." She took a sip of her juice, closing her eyes and relishing in the flavor of pink lemonade.

The pastor's office was well air conditioned and quite cozy. The chair's seat seemed to mold to her butt and allowed her to be comfortable. She looked around and noted he had all kinds of books, and his degrees covered one wall. She picked up the picture on his desk of him and his family.

"Well, Zivial, if you aren't here for yourself, then who are you here for?"

Tiny continued to look at the picture without looking up at him. "I'm here in regards of Amber."

She had to jerk her chair backward so the juice he was drinking didn't spill all over her as he spit it out and damn near sprayed her in the process.

"I'm sorry about that." He began wiping it up with Kleenexes from the box on his desk. After he finished, he sat back down and scooted closer to his desk. "Now, tell me what's wrong with Amber?"

Tiny shook her head. "Well, first of all, I just found out she is only 16 years old, and all those months we stayed together she was on the run from her family."

She looked over at the pastor. His eyes were so big she thought they would pop out and roll across his desk. He started to loosen his tie and fan his face in a mock attempt to gain some sort of relief.

"Can you imagine how stupid I felt when the

cops ran up on me and said I was harboring a juvenile runaway? I felt humiliated. And that was only the beginning, because they hauled me into the station and questioned me, asking where we'd been for the last past months. It took everything I had to make up the story that I did. After it was all said and done, they still had their sights on charging me." She lowered her head and shook it.

The pastor had unbuttoned three buttons on his shirt by now, and there was sweat running down his face. He kept fidgeting in his chair. His eyes were scanning the entire room as if he were looking for an escape route.

"Pastor, did you know how old she was?" Tiny asked, barely above a whisper.

He shook his head so hard she could have sworn she heard a bone pop. "No, sister, I swear I didn't. Had I known she was that old, I would have found out who her parents were and made sure they came and got her. That's my word, too."

"What about the sex, though?"

He inhaled so hard his chair scooted backward. "Sex, sister? What are you talking about, sex? There was no sex between us. I'm married, and I'm the pastor of this church. Shame on you!"

Tiny frowned. "Are you sure about that?"

He nodded. "I most certainly am. I love my wife, and I love my family. I would not do anything to jeopardize the integrity or the sanctity of my marriage."

It took every ounce of maturity Tiny had within to not break out laughing in his face. If she had not witnessed firsthand some of the things that took place between him and Amber, she would have sworn he was telling the truth, and there would not have been anyone who could have convinced her otherwise.

She listened to him go on and on about why he would not sin against his family or the church. He was just about to pick up the Bible and start quoting scriptures when she stopped him. She held up her hand and he stopped, feeling as if he had gotten his point across.

"Listen, pastor, what you did for me was a good thing. You took me in off the streets and gave me a place to lay my head. You put food into my stomach. You allowed me to wash my body every single day. For those things, I am most grateful. I do not want to bring any trouble your way. You're obviously an important man." She stood up and paced back and forth in front of his desk with her arms folded behind her back.

The pastor looked on in silence. Tiny was trying to rile up the nerve to be able to complete the next portion of her plan. A part of her felt conflicted. She really didn't want to hurt the pastor. After all, she thought of him as a fairly good man. He had done all of those things she had mentioned. The thought still came to her head and left her in wonder as to why he never came at her in a sexual way. She wondered if she wasn't his type or something. Maybe he just went for exotic women, or white girls altogether. She shrugged her shoulders. That wasn't important. Sometimes she hated having A.D.D. because it caused her mind to often lose its train of thought. She shook the cobwebs out of her head, and tried to focus in on the task at hand.

"Zivial, are we done here? Have I proven myself to you?" he asked, turning his head sideways like a puppy.

Tiny stopped in her tracks and let out a loud sigh. "Pastor Harold, I'm just gon' be honest with you. Amber is pregnant, and I know it's your baby because you're the only one she was with. I can vouch for that. She's fallen in love with you, and the only person that knows about the baby outside of you and her is me."

He interrupted. "A baby? What are you saying? I have never touched that girl, I swear to it."

Tiny held her hand up. "Stop it. I was there on several occasions and watched you two in action. For a preacher, you sure got a filthy mind. You did some things to her that even make me ashamed, and I'm a free spirit." She gave him a look of disgust. "Now, what I want to talk about is how you're going to help me better my situation."

His eyes went from staring at the floor to shooting invisible daggers at her. "Money! I should've known a harlot like you had some sort of an agenda." He curled up his face.

Tiny slapped her hand on her hip. "Or would you rather I just go to the police and they can drag you off to prison for taking advantage of a minor? A white minor, at that. Let's not forget the most important part of the equation."

He shot up from his chair. "And what is it you want from me? What do you need, some weed money? You want to go and get your fake hair done? Or do you want to go and spend some money so that Jordan gets richer? What do you want, sister girl?" he said with strong sarcasm and spite.

If Tiny felt bad about blackmailing him before, she felt no pity at all now. So that was how he thought of her, as some ghetto hoodrat who spent her money on weaves, marijuana, and Jordans. She felt so offended she wanted to lash out and punch him.

She wondered if she did look like the average hood rat, though. She wondered if that was how the world viewed her. Did she give off the impression she would never go farther than the slums of Chicago? When people looked at her, did they see an average statistic? Did she give off the "straight ghetto" vibe?

Secretly, she had never envisioned leaving Chicago's projects or doing anything positive with her life because she didn't think she could. She always thought it was meant for her to be exactly where she was. She felt people like her weren't meant to do anything positive, or be anyone great. With thoughts going on in her head like that all day long, it made it hard to love herself.

"You know what, pastor? You're going to help me enroll into the Technical College downtown. Not only that, but you're going to foot the bill. You're also going to be getting me a car, an apartment just as good as the one you got for Amber, and you're going to furnish it."

He started to interrupt, but she kept on going.

"Let me finish. I'm not finished yet." She rolled her eyes. "You're also going to give me an allowance every two weeks and help me get a good job by using your connections. I am looking to better myself, and you're going to use some of this church money you're siphoning out of the flock to help me do it."

He walked up on her so close she could smell his aftershave. "Little girl, if you don't get your li'l ghetto self out of my office making the ridiculous requests, I'm gon' remove you." He sucked his teeth. "Ain't nobody gon' believe you or that white girl. What, they just gon' take your word for it? All the sudden you're the saint and I'm the beast? Child, please. It's my word against yours, so who you think they gon' believe, me or some project kid?" He laughed so loud his Adam's apple moved up and down.

"So, that's how you want to play things, huh?" Tiny sat down on his desk, turned a piece of paper over and wrote her demands on it. Then she rummaged through her purse until she located the first tape. She walked over to the VCR attached to the television in his room. "Do you mind?"

"Please, be my guest, but after this I want you to leave."

She nodded. "No problem. Now keep in mind, this is only the first of fifteen, I'm actually going to let you keep this one because I've made a copy of it." She pushed in the tape and turned on the TV, setting it to channel three.

As soon as she set the channel, the moaning started, and then on the screen the pastor and Amber came into view. He lay on his back while Amber rode him in slow motion.

Tiny looked over her shoulder at him and

smiled. "I never told you that you have a nice body for an older man."

The pastor could not believe his eyes. "How did you get this? Where were you? I don't understand. I didn't know how old she was, I swear it."

On screen, he placed Amber on all fours and pummeled her from the back while she called herself his dirty little whore. He pulled on her hair and spanked her behind, all the while he wore his red tie.

Tiny spun on her toes and walked up to him. "This is one of the tapes that turn me on the most. I love the way you're manhandling her. Look at how you pull her hair and throw her around that bed as if she's a rag doll." She was standing in his face now.

The pastor looked as if he had caught food poisoning. He felt sick and like his life was about to be over. He was caught, there was no faking about that. She had him just where she wanted him, and in order for him to maintain his life, he would have to play by her rules.

Tiny stepped one foot closer until she had her head pressed to his chest. "You know, why does this have to be a bad thing? Why can't you just take care of me and help me get to where I need to be, and we leave it at that? You're thousands and thousands of dollars ahead every Sunday, you get that tax free from these people who believe in you. I'm trying to get my life on track so I can begin to believe in me. Is that so wrong?"

She ran her hand down and then up his pant leg until she was cupping his crotch. She felt his pole and squeezed.

"Zivial, what are you doing?" he asked as he stood on tip-toe.

She was already unbuckling his belt and pulling his pants down. She dropped to her knees along with them, reached up and pulled his boxers down. His penis sprung into the air like a brown baseball bat. She reached up, stroking it.

He closed his eyes and tried to focus on what her hand was doing. In the background he and Amber moaned and groaned on screen. He couldn't help opening his eyes to see himself giving it to her good from behind. Her breasts shook on her small frame. Below him, Tiny jerked his manhood back and forth.

Tiny didn't know what was turning her on more. Was it the fact she was almost sure he would submit to her demands, and from now on she would not have to worry about going without? She would be able to choose a career path for herself, and it would all be paid for and sponsored by a religious pervert who – for the most part – had a good heart, but couldn't control his sexual desires.

Or maybe it was the tape in general that had her so hot. The first time she had watched it alone she made herself shake and tremble three times and couldn't even look Amber in the eye the next day. There was nothing more sexy than a man who took charge in the bedroom. It was her weakness.

She looked up at him at the same time he slid into her mouth. She gripped his penis tight and dragged her lips up and down it, making loud, wet noises. She felt like she was on fire, full of desire and pent-up lust. She had not been intimate in a very long time, and it was starting to eat at her. She speared her head onto his piece at full speed, and just when she thought he was ready to release, she stopped and stood up.

The pastor's eyes shot open. "What, why did you stop? Please keep going?" he said with a voice full of lust and frustration.

She nodded. "Do we have a deal?" She grabbed his penis and kept on stroking it.

His eyes rolled into the back of his head as he humped into her hand. In that moment nothing else mattered. So, he would have to spend money on her to keep her silent, and he would be putting her through school. None of that mattered. He felt a little respect for her on the way she played her cards, and if he could also get some of that ghetto booty, that would make things a million times better. He had lusted after her for a long time, but never had the balls to approach her. He also feared her because her family was so deeply rooted within the church. But quiet as he kept, he felt she was probably one of the sexiest females he had ever seen.

He nodded. "Okay, we have a deal. I'll take care of you just as long as you keep this between us, and you keep me safe from them white folks. What about the baby?"

"You'll take care of it from a distance. I don't want you to let Amber know that I know. Things will stay the same way they are. If I find out you told her anything, all bets are off, and I'll be forced to do what I gotta do. Do you understand me?"

He stabbed forward, trying to feel her hand

again. "Yeah, you have my word."

She leaned down and licked his head. "Alright, I want you to take me right here, right now. I want you to do me like you did her on that tape." She reached under her skirt and pulled her panties down and off her right foot.

The pastor didn't have to be told twice. He knocked her to the floor, flipped her onto her stomach, then pulled her up by her hips. She reached behind herself and found his manhood and slid it between her sex lips. He pushed forward, and from there on took her like she had never given him permission.

Chapter 12

One day after coming home from enrolling in cosmetology school, Tiny came home to find Brandy sitting on the couch along with Jaheim, a belt wrapped around her arm and her brother slowly sliding a syringe into her veins. Beside them, Amber nodded in and out with saliva dripping off of her chin. As they heard the door close, they looked up at where she stood in a state of disbelief.

Jaheim paid her no mind, he pushed down on the feeder, driving the poison deep into his sister's veins. Tiny watched as Brandy's eyes slowly rolled to the back of her head. She popped her lips and ran her hand across her face.

Beside her, Amber was scratching the skin away from her shoulder. She smiled, and then frowned, and then appeared to be snoring, and then wide awake all at the same time. Her hair was a mess, and she had on the same clothes she had worn three days in a row already.

Tiny became concerned about the child living within her womb. She knew the girl had a cocaine addiction, and she smoked weed. Now that she was adding in heroin, the baby living inside her had no chance. She felt bad for her friend. She also became concerned because Amber was the epicenter of what she had going on. She needed her to keep a level head so she could cash in on her and the pastor's relationship. He still thought she was only 16 years old, when in actuality she was closer to 20. She just looked young for her age, which had worked in Tiny's favor.

Tiny sat down on the couch beside her and put her arm over her shoulder. "Amber, are you okay, girl? When did you start shooting that heroin in you? Don't you know you're pregnant?" she whispered in her ear.

Amber opened her eyes, which were so hazy they looked like she'd polished them with baby oil. Her lips were white and crusty. Her hair was tangled and smelled like a wet dog. She was sweating profusely, and Tiny could even smell her womanhood. She was ripe and due for a shower.

"Come on, girl, let's get you into the tub. You smell horrible," Tiny said, pulling on one of her arms to get her to stand up.

Amber tried to fight her off. "No, I don't feel like it. I just want to sit here and groove, man. I'm in heaven, and you're ruining it." She ran her tongue across her lips.

Her breath smelled like the stairwell in the projects. It made Tiny's stomach turn. She tried to pull her up again, and this time she came with her.

She sat her down in the tub and ran the water around her after stripping all her clothes away and throwing them in the garbage. As soon as she removed her panties, the whole bathroom lit up with the aroma of spoiled fish. It was so loud Tiny could barely breathe. As the water began to fill the tub, it became thick with a gray, cloudy substance. The substance floated to the side of the tub and pasted itself against the rim. All Tiny could do was shake her head as she felt her eyes become watery.

She squirted the body wash into the loofa, worked up some suds, and then proceeded to wash her friend's whole body. She shampooed her hair, and even conditioned it, then took the spray nozzle and rinsed her off.

She made her stand up, then reached down and unplugged the drain and turned the shower on. "Okay, Amber, now you take a nice shower, and I'm gon' be right here waiting for you when you're done." She pulled the curtain and started cleaning up the bathroom.

After a while, she could make out the sobbing of Amber. This made her blink tears. She could only imagine what was going on inside her friend's mind. Surely she was aware she was throwing her life away, allowing herself to be under Jaheim's control. She was slowly falling into the abyss. The sobs kept getting louder and louder until they turned into a scream, and then Tiny heard her fall.

She rushed to the tub and pulled the curtains away. What she saw made her run to the toilet and purge her guts. She flushed, wiped her mouth off on a damp rag, and then ran back to the tub. Amber lay on her back with her legs wide open, and between them a pool of blood and the head of her baby. Tiny nearly fainted.

She ran to the phone and called 911 and told them to hurry. The whole time Jaheim kept asking her what the matter was. She brushed him off and told him to go look in the bathroom. Brandy sat on the couch, drawing heroin into her syringe, getting ready to take another dose. She was oblivious as to what was going on around her. She simply seemed like she didn't care.

Tiny ran all around the apartment, trying to

make it look presentable. There was so much drug paraphernalia she worried about all of them being hauled into jail. They had a white girl in the bathtub with blood all around her and a baby's head sticking out of her vagina.

Jaheim came out of the bathroom with his eyes bucked. He looked scared. "What the fuck do we do? How are we going to get her to the hospital? I'm not sticking my hand in that tub around all that damn blood. Did you see that the baby is coming out of her?" He was talking a mile a minute.

Tiny walked up on him and backhanded him so hard he fell to the couch holding his face. He had even let out a little yelp.

"Shut the hell up! You take Brandy and y'all get the fuck out of here, because I called the police. And they are going to be here quick, because we are on Lake Shore Drive. This is a white neighborhood, so if they see three black people and one white girl in a pool of blood, you know somebody going to jail, and I already know you got warrants."

He nodded stupidly. "Okay, we gon' go. We gon' go right now. Come on, Brandy."

Brandy snatched her arm away from him. "I ain't! I'm too high right now. I feel good, daddy." She laid back on the couch and rubbed her stomach, popping her lips.

He frowned down on her. "You what? I know you ain't say no, bitch!" He pulled her up by her hair and dragged her across the floor toward the door.

"Alright! Alright, just stop! Let me go, I can walk on my own! You're blowing my high, man!"

she said, fighting to get his fingers out of her hair.

"Well, let's go, then. I ain't playing with you. This bitch called the police, and if they take me to jail, I'm gon' kick your ass, I swear to God."

She climbed to her feet with her hair looking a mess. She was starting to look 30 years old already. "Why you go and do that for, Tiny? Damn. I thought you was my friend," she slurred, rocking back and forth on her feet.

Tiny opened the door and held it until they left. She then finished cleaning up their mess, hoping for better days.

***

"I see you're going to insist on breaking me. Why can't you get something simple, like a sports car? How is a little something like you going to handle an SUV?" the pastor asked Tiny seriously.

They had traveled all the way to Indiana just so he could purchase her the car she wanted. Tiny felt he didn't want to be seen in the city of Chicago with her, and that didn't bother her one bit. The only thing that mattered to her was that she got the Eddie Bauer truck she had been lusting over ever since she saw it on television.

She didn't pay him any mind. When she saw it across the lot, she ran to it at full speed. He jogged behind her and couldn't help laughing at her enthusiasm. She stood in front of the hood of the truck and pointed. "That's it right there. That's the one I want. I have to have it." She walked along the side and opened the driver's door and climbed in.

The truck made her feel so small, yet secure, and that's exactly what she was going for. She sniffed the air and smiled. She fell in love with the wood grain dash, the leather seats, the nice CD player with the detachable face, and it even had a navigation system. This was hers, it had to be.

The pastor climbed into the passenger's seat. "So this is what you want, huh?" He placed his hand on her thigh and squeezed.

She nodded and spread her knees. "This is me right here. I still want you to put a little music in it for me, but other than that it's perfect."

She felt his fingers enter her. He was just starting the motion when the salesman walked up to the truck. He drug his fingers out of her body and sucked them into his mouth. She couldn't help but laugh at him.

The fat black man with an all-black Armani suit came to the driver's side window. "I take it you've found what you're looking for?" he said, already tasting the commission that was sure to come. He looked from Tiny to the pastor.

"Yep, we sure have. This is it right here. It's black on black and perfect." She looked over her shoulder to the pastor.

"Well, I guess we should go and take care of the paperwork. Is there a place we can talk?"

"Right this way."

***

Tiny didn't think things could get any better for her. She had already completed a semester at the technical college, and she already had a job lined up. The pastor had gotten her connected with a woman who owned a chain of beauty salons throughout the city, and she had promised to give her a chair at one of her shops as long as Tiny agreed to finish getting her degrees and she could muster up her own clientele, which wouldn't be a problem because the pastor had recommended her to the entire youth choir at the church. She promised them 10 percent off of their bill, and one-by-one all twenty of them, even the boys, signed on to be her customers.

She had a knack for doing hair. She specialized in micro braids, perms, weaves, and even curls. When it came to the boys, most of them wanted curls or hair cuts, so she whipped them to the best of her ability. Before she knew it, her name was ringing and she had people coming from all over the city to sit in her chair. This made her feel good about herself, and she became somewhat optimistic about the future.

She had been working on the job for three months when Avery walked in and tapped her on the shoulder. "Say there, pretty lady, you got room for me?" he asked, smiling.

She turned around and gave him a look of shock. She threw her arms around him, hugging tightly. "Hey there, long time no see. I thought you had forgotten all about me," she said, sweeping up her station after cutting a little boy's hair. He had cried the whole time because it was his first cut. This made his mother cry, and Tiny followed suit. It felt like a disaster, but when it was all said and done she had hooked him up.

He shook his head. "Nall, it wasn't never nothing like that. To be honest with you, I'm just getting out of jail. I got knocked out west collecting from this pimp. I ain't know he had called the police before I got there. They caught me with a pistol and a few bags. I just bonded out. So, shit been real hectic. I ain't never forgot about you, though. How could I?" He looked her up and down and bit into his bottom lip at the sight of how the capris hugged her ample bottom.

She laughed. "Uh-huh." She looked him over. "Damn, you do look rough, though. How about you sit on down in my chair and I'll hook you up. This way I can pay you back for that pizza, and I can find out what's good with you. Bet?"

He nodded. "Yeah, that sound like a plan. I want you to cut these dreads off, too. I'm about to turn over a new leaf. I just got an offer from my cousin, King," he said, sitting in the chair and taking the rubber band out of his hair that held it in a ponytail.

Tiny shook out the apron and placed it over his body. "What King is you talking about?" She ran her fingers through his dreads and thought they may need to be washed first. "We gon' wash your hair before I cut it? When was the last time you did it?"

He shrugged his shoulders. "I don't know. You know you ain't supposed to be washing your hair when you living the dread life. You're a beautician, you definitely should know better than that."

She leaned him over the sink after setting the temperature to the right degrees. "Boy, somebody done told you wrong. It's true you're supposed to not wash it as much while it's dreading up, but after it's dreaded you're supposed to wash it as much as possible to keep it healthy and strong. That's why so many people's hair breaks off. It's because their roots are dying from the damage."

After he had been under the dryer for 20 minutes, she sat him back down and began cutting his dreads off. "So, tell me about this King."

"Like I was saying, that's my cousin, my father's sister's son. He doing it big out there. I know you just heard about how he took over the Robert Taylor Homes from that nigga Draylon. He just did the same thing to the Ada B Wells, and him and his crew the Young Radicals doing numbers throughout the city. They got this heroin that once you shoot it, you get so addicted to it that can't nothing else get you as high. They say it make you feel like your first time every time you take it. It's crazy money being made, and he just gave me a slot. I could gross 10 Gs a day." At this he smiled, showing off his dimples.

Tiny was spinning him all around in the chair, working her magic. She had heard about King and his organization. From what she had been told, they were relentless, cold-blooded killers who had the mayor in their back pocket. There was no way they could do the things they were doing if they didn't have immunity. Very few people rolled around the city in Corvettes and Ferraris. She had heard King was the first black man in Chicago to have been fully accepted by the head of the Five Mafia Families.

"Yo, I think that's cool, but are you sure you

know what you're doing? I heard your cousin has a lot of enemies and a whole lot of bodies on his hands."

Avery laughed out loud. "Yeah, bro been knocking shit down. But it's all good, though, because he can't be touched. It's money to be made, and I'm about to get mines."

She finished his cut and spun him around so he could see himself in the mirror.

He ran his hand across the top of his head. "That's what I'm talking about. You hooked me up, ma. Yo, I gotta hit your hand for this." He pulled out a huge knot and pulled her off two $100 bills.

She pushed his hand away. "Nall, I'm cool. I told you I owed you for that time you picked me up off that expressway. I appreciated that," she said, rubbing the pomade in between her hands and then onto the top of his head. "This right here is a grease that's gon' help your hair wave up. Once you get that whole wave thing going, yo' gon' be something to look at. Hold on one second." She grabbed the hair clippers and touched up his edge and stood back. "All right, now you good."

He laughed. "What you mean, *then* I'm gon' be something to look at?" He raised an eyebrow at her. "You hurt my feelings by that comment. I thought I looked pretty good already."

She grunted. "I mean, you a'ight," she said, teasing him. He grabbed her arm and pulled her close to him. There were a few women in the store who had their heads under hair dryers who could not take their eyes off of them. Tiny politely shook out of his grasp once she noted the stares. That wasn't the professional way to be carrying on, and she knew she should have been behaving more appropriately.

"Avery, I'm at work. I can't be carrying on like that," she said, slightly above a whisper.

He grabbed his chin and looked around. "Aw, damn, my bad. I wasn't even thinking."

She smiled, looking up at him. He was a sight to see. Tall, dark-skinned with a nice cut physique just like she liked them to be. She started to picture how he would look naked and felt a tingle shoot through her.

He looked down on her. "Tiny, why don't you kick it with me tonight. Let's just hit up the city, see a movie and get something to eat. What you think about that?"

She had promised Amber she would visit her that night at the rehab center. Ever since the day she had found her in the bathtub with her baby partially out of her, the girl had decided to clean up her act. She's checked into an inpatient treatment facility where she struggled to become a better her. Tiny knew in order for her to get over the hump, she would need her constant support.

"Avery, I would love to kick it with you tonight, but I already made prior arrangements."

He lowered his head. "Aw, some nigga already got you booked in for the night?" He dusted his pants off and put a cigar behind his ear. Checking himself in the mirror one last time, he prepared to leave.

"Nall, it ain't nothing like that. Right now I'm not seeing anybody, and I would really like to be with you after I leave here, but it's just that my homegirl going through this whole rehab thing, and I have to be there to support her as much as I can. Now, if you want to roll with me out to Markum, you could chill in the car for about 45 minutes while I holler at her. Or you can just come through around 8:00 and we could get together then." She looked up at him.

"Yo, that's cool. Just give me the address and I'll call you when I'm on my way."

***

Tiny always hated coming to see her friend in such a state. It always reminded her that Amber could have been her, because she once followed behind the same directions of Jaheim. She silently thanked God that He had been so kind to have saved her from a similar fate. He had a plan for her, she was sure of that. She just didn't know exactly what it was yet.

She had witnessed her friend go through so much. After the medics picked her up and whisked her away to the hospital, she had nearly lost her baby. She gave birth inside of the ambulance, and the baby was born with a faint heartbeat. Just on the way to the hospital alone, the baby had died and come back three times.

If that wasn't bad enough, in the midst of Amber giving birth to her baby girl, her body reacted to the process by trying to rid itself of the drugs, and she wound up seizing and going into a slight overdose.

Ever since the day Ariana was born, she had been hooked up to tubes. Born addicted to heroin and cocaine on top of being premature was a huge battle for any child to face. The little girl was strong, though, and getting stronger. She had already gotten the heroin monkey off of her back. She was also starting to grow bigger, which was a blessing.

Tiny shuffled around uncomfortably in her seat and awaited Amber. The last time she had seen her was two weeks prior, and all she did was cry the whole time. She prayed she was feeling better and she wouldn't have to sit through another meltdown. Times like those always left her greatly depressed, and she had too much on her plate to be laying somewhere in bed, refusing to get out because her depression was getting the better of her.

She just wanted to let Amber know she had her back and be on her way. She stopped by the hospital every day to see Ariana because it was only a few blocks from the salon. Amber no longer had custody of her. She had been taken by the state of Illinois. Amber was to undergo treatment before she could be considered eligible to gain custody.

When she saw Amber making her way toward where she was sitting on the couch in front of the big screen television, she stood up and opened her arms. Amber ran into them and hugged her tightly, already sobbing. They sat down on the couch at the same time, with Tiny brushing Amber's hair away from her face. She looked like she had lost more weight. Tiny could actually see the bones in her face clearly now. The last time Tiny had been there, she confessed she had not eaten in a few days. Tiny hoped that wasn't the case this time.

She placed her head onto her shoulder.

"Amber, baby, how have you been?"

Amber picked her head up. "I don't know, sis. I think I'm starting to feel worse than I ever have. I'm not going to even lie to you, either. I used."

Tiny pushed her back to look at her face more clearly. "You what? How is that even possible? You're in a rehab center. Where did you get some dope from?" Tiny asked, livid.

Amber ran her hand over her lips and swallowed. "I got it from a friend here."

Tiny frowned. "A friend, are you fucking serious? Does your friend know you have a daughter who's fighting for her life who needs you? Does your friend know Child Protective Services has her and they plan on keeping her until you get clean, or if you don't get clean within the next few months they are going to take her for good? Does your friend know all of that?" Tiny looked at her in anger.

Amber wrapped her arms around herself and lowered her head. "No, she doesn't know all of that. We were both just breaking down so much about our situation when she gave up the stuff, and it is so good, too. They call it the Virgin, and it's the best dope I have ever had in my life. I didn't feel any pain while I was on it. I had no worries. I was in another dimension; this world of pain did not exist."

Tiny could not believe what she was hearing. "Are you fucking kidding me right now? Are you really sitting here telling me how good some fucking dope is when your little girl is in the hospital fighting for her life? What the fuck is your problem, Amber? Have you really lost your mind?" She reached and turned her chin so she could look into her eyes. "Are you giving up?"

Amber lowered her head as tears sailed down her cheeks. She shrugged her shoulders and swallowed. Her lips had turned a crusty white, and the sweater she wore was two times too big for her now, when in the past it clung to her body. She looked as if she was fading away.

She wiped a tear away. "I don't know what I'm doing anymore. I don't even know if I want to live, much less if I want a kid to be responsible for. I'm not strong enough to take care of her. What am I supposed to do?"

Tiny leaned into her face. "You're supposed to fight through and be a mother to that child you brought into this world. She didn't ask to be here. You made her, and God blessed you with her. Now it's your responsibility to woman up and quit being a little girl and so fucking selfish. I really don't understand you. You would go out night after night and bust your ass for that dope fiend Jaheim because you loved him, but you turn your back on your daughter, your own flesh and blood."

"I don't need you to tell me what I'm doing wrong, Zivial. Why don't you get off of your high horse? You are no better than me," she spat.

"And you know what? I never said I was. I am only saying these things to you because I care about you, and I know you are stronger than you are putting on. You have to live up to your potential and fight hard for what you want to obtain. Nothing is given, everything is earned, sister. Now, if you are trying to tell me you need help, then here I am."

Amber shook her head hard. "No, that's not it. I'm telling you I don't want to be a mother. I don't want to be responsible for that little girl because I will do nothing but fail her. I don't know the first thing about being a mother."

Tiny grabbed her hand. "So we learn together, and we raise her to be a prominent, strong young woman of values. We lead her down a path opposite of the ones we came down. We believe in her and fight with her to become whatever her heart desires. Through her we gain a second chance."

Amber sat silently. "Zivial, I'm tired of living. I don't think I'm going to be able to make it through the week. I'm tired of being on this earth. There is nothing but pain here, and the only time I feel like I can survive is when heroin is in my system. I literally need it." Snot dripped from her nose. She wiped it away with her sleeve. "I know that sounds horrible, but I am telling you the truth. I am ruined, and there is no more good inside of me. I have to give up this fight because I am losing round after round. And it hurts me worst being here and trying to fight when I know I will lose the battle. Can you understand that?"

Tiny didn't know what to say. She had so many conflicting emotions going through her that she felt stuck. "I don't know what to say to you, Amber. I mean, I could sit here and try to preach to you what's the right things to do, but clearly that won't work because you already have your mind made up.

I mean, I feel sorry for you and even worse for Ariana, because you really are a beautiful person and she deserves to have a relationship with you. I don't know why it's so hard for you to believe in yourself, and I don't know what more I can do to help you. Do you?"

Amber shook her head. "No, I don't think I can be helped."

Tiny felt the tears welling up in her eyes. "Damn, Amber, I just wish you would fight." The well had been broken. "So, what about Ariana? What do we do about her?" Tiny asked, her voice breaking up and tears streaming down her cheeks so bad the front of her blouse was soaked.

"Please take care of her for me. Let her know I wasn't strong enough to enter into her life. Tell her I will protect her from above or below, or wherever I wind up." She sniffed the mucous back inside of her nose. "Tell her I wanted her to have a good life."

Tiny fell to her knees, holding Amber's hand. She rocked back and forth, sobbing. "No, sister, you tell her all these things. You're supposed to fight for her like no one fought for us. How can you give up? How can you leave us behind?" Tiny wailed at the top of her lungs.

Amber snatched her hands out of her grasp and walked away from the couch.

***

That night she had called Avery and canceled. At 2:30 a.m. she received a call from the rehabilitation center. Amber had slit both of her wrists and locked herself into a bathroom, where she bled out before any help could arrive.

Tiny broke down. She promised herself she would do what she could for Ariana. No matter what she would have to go through, she would be there for her.

Chapter 13

"I'm still trying to wrap my head around the fact we're about to fly on a private jet. You're either playing with my emotions, or this is a dream I pray I don't wake up from," she said, stepping onto the jet with her Gucci luggage.

It was hell to get Lena to allow her to take a full week off for a vacation Avery had sprung on her out of the blue. Getting time off from school was no problem because they were on a three-week break, but Lena knew a week without Tiny meant one of her salons would lose money.

Tiny had assured her she should not worry. She had scheduled all of her appointments for the week when she returned, so she in fact would not be losing any money at all. The two days prior to the trip she had been so busy with customers because they were aware of her upcoming trip and they wanted to be squeezed in, so most of the money was already salvaged, and the rest she would take care of when she returned.

After breaking this down to Lena, she finally got it and gave her the nod. Tiny had helped her business boom, so she could relent to her taking a vacation. She deserved it. She even offered to give her some money to take along on the trip, which Tiny accepted.

She and Avery had grown closer over the last few months after Amber passed away. He was a strong shoulder to lean on, and whenever she called him, he would always come running for her. That made her feel good.

As much time as they spent together, they still had yet to be together intimately. It seemed like every time she felt it was the right time, something came up, so she chalked it up as maybe it wasn't meant to be as of yet.

"Like I told you before, woman, you ain't dreaming. I ain't playing with your emotions. This is real, and you about to be in the air in a few minutes. But it's also like I told you: a part of this trip has a lot to do with business. I have to take care of that first for King, and then we're free to do us." She saw him set the three duffle bags down and push them under the seats way in the back.

The plane looked like a small VIP section of a nightclub. The interior was champagne colored, and there were bottles of Moet sitting on ice. As soon as they stepped onto the plane, two beautiful exotic flight attendants began attending to their every beck and call. Tiny smiled and thought she could get used to that.

They settled into the middle of the plane, where there was a big screen television and all-white leather seats. A big bowl of weed was placed in front of them, and as Tiny sat in one of the chairs it proceeded to massage her entire body. She closed her eyes and smiled as she felt the plane hitting the runway and taking flight.

Avery kissed her on the forehead. "You feeling good, li'l momma?"

She smiled. "About as good as I possibly can. Why, you got something up your sleeve that's gon' make me feel better?" She said all of this without opening her eyes.

Before she could even finish her sentence, she felt two sets of lips sucking on her neck, and then she felt a hand on her breasts, dipping inside the Fendi top she had on. Her eyes shot open just as one of the flight attendants slipped to her knees and pushed her dress up. Tiny spread her thighs and the woman's head disappeared. All she could feel was her sucking her sex through her panties while the other female kissed her and pulled on her nipples.

Avery held two Moet bottles in the air and did a little dance. From the speakers 2Pac rapped about thug passion, and Tiny lay back with her thighs spread so wide she looked like she was doing a gymnastics trick while both women feasted on her body and brought her off again and again as they flew over the United States.

***

By the time they landed in San Juan, Puerto Rico, she was exhausted, and Avery had not even touched her. The two exotic beauties had done everything imaginable to her while he sat back and watched. She came so many times she lost count. After the women put her to sleep, they worked on Avery. She woke up to find him manhandling both ladies, and for an entire hour she enjoyed the show.

They arrived at Hotel De Ponce at 5:00 p.m. and were met by a stretch Lincoln Navigator limousine. Two beefy Puerto Rican guards grabbed their bags and loaded them into the stretch. Tiny could tell they were packing. The fronts of their shirts were poked out, and she could make out the handles of each weapon. That made her feel a bit uneasy. She held on tightly to Avery's arm as they went from the limo to their grand suite.

It was so big she could have sworn they were in some kind of a movie. The entire place was all white, and she could tell it was rich with heritage as statues aligned the walls, and below them a backstory.

The place was absolutely beautiful, and the atmosphere alone made her feel like a queen. Avery dropped the duffle bags onto the floor and took his shirt off. He walked back to the big double doors and closed them as the guards gave him a nod and told him they would be outside if he needed anything.

He unzipped one of the bags and Tiny saw it was filled with stacks and stacks of money. He reached into it and pulled out a huge gun and screwed something on the end of it. "Look ma, I'm about to go take care of some business. Why don't you take a shower, or sit in the Jacuzzi for a while? I'll be back in a few hours, and then we can see what this city is all about. I got a feeling you gon' love San Juan. This is a beautiful place, rich in culture. My mother was born here." He slipped a black vest on and then he put his shirt over that. "I'll be back in a minute."

She watched him walk out of the big doors, then they closed again. Being a girl from the projects, the first thing she thought about was the fact she had seen bundles and bundles of money in one of the bags. Her curiosity got the better of her. She dropped to her knees and unzipped the bag before she could stop herself.

Sure enough, there it was again. Bundles and bundles of $100 bills rubber banded. Her eyes damn near rolled out of her head. She could not believe there was so much money. She crawled to her right and unzipped the other two as well, and they also were filled up with money. She quickly zipped them back, though she felt the urge to stuff a few bundles into her suitcase. She literally had to start praying to Jesus for strength to not do it. She put everything back like he had left it and took a deep breath. There had to be some sort of an explanation for carrying around so much money, even though she already knew what it was. The private plane, the bundles of money, the beefy guards, the guns. Sure as shit stank, they were either purchasing drugs or paying for the drugs that were already in Chicago.

King was a major dude, everybody knew that, and if Avery was working for him, which he clearly was, then he was due to be making some major moves that would involve a lot of money. She just hoped everything went according to plan, because they were a long way from home.

She opened the doors that led to the balcony and stepped onto it, looking down at the narrow street. The humidity was scorching and through the roof. Down below, a little Puerto Rican man pushed his cart up and down the streets selling his popsicles. She wanted one so bad she felt like climbing down and buying one. Her balcony wasn't that far from the cobbled street below.

She called down to him. "Say, señor." She went into her bra and pulled out a $5.00 bill and waved it at him.

He looked up at her and waved. "Jess, ju wanna poppa sickle, liddle lade?"

She nodded and waved the five dollar bill again.

He pulled two out of his cart and rolled it up under her balcony. He stood on tippy-toe to hand it to her, but he couldn't quite reach. He looked around and then upward, placed the popsicles in his waistband, and started to climb up the balcony.

Tiny felt giddy. She was dying to taste the iced fruit juice. She could not wait until she had it in her hands and was tearing off the wrapper. It was all she could think about.

The man was grunting below her, climbing up the rocky side of the hotel, when all of a sudden she heard a man yell, then a car came flying down the street and slammed on its brakes. Two small females jumped out of the car with long, flowing curly hair. They ran over to the climbing man and pulled him down. He crashed to the cobblestone beneath him, then another female opened the back door to the car and ran over to them with a golf club in her hands. As soon as she got to the other two and the man, she swung it and connected with the back of his head, knocking him off of his feet. They then dragged him from under the balcony and stomped him for five minutes straight.

Tiny looked on in a state of pure shock and horror. She didn't know why they would do such a thing, and she became fearful and wondered if she was next. She slowly backed away from the balcony toward the entrance to the room when one of the females called up to her.

"Hey, are you okay, Tiny?"

Tiny? Did the woman just call her by her name? This was really starting to freak her out. She watched the woman jog over to her balcony and stand under it.

She tried to compose herself. "Yeah, I'm good. How do you know my name?"

The woman smiled. "You're a guest of King. You're protected here. That man is not what you think he is. He is a bandit who preys on innocent people from the mainland. Look at this." She walked back over to him, took the popsicles out of his waistband, and tore the paper away from one of them only to reveal a dagger. "Do you understand now? If we would have let him climb your balcony, he would have raped and possibly killed you. Afterward your possessions would have become his."

Tiny's mind was totally blown away. Here she was, moments away from being a victim. She had been stupid enough to allow some random man to climb onto her balcony all so she could get what appeared to be a popsicle. What if he had robbed her and taken all of the money Avery had left in the room? How would she have explained that to him? Even worse, what would King have done to the both of them?

She looked down onto the beautiful woman. "I thank you so much. How could I ever repay you?"

She waved her away dismissively. "Never mind that. You be more careful and enjoy the island. There are a million more people here that are just like him, so you have to be wise and don't trust anybody. Stay close to Avery and keep your doors locked at all times." After saying this she waved, and she and her two companions left without saying another word.

Tiny looked down on the man who lay in the street with blood leaking from his skull. She thought maybe she should call for a paramedic or something, but decided against it. She stepped back inside and locked the doors. Minutes later, she was seated in the Jacuzzi with the event weighing heavily on her mind.

Avery returned sometime later that night while she lay in the bed watching old Good Times reruns on the big screen. She found it awfully funny a piece of Chicago had made it all the way out onto the island of Puerto Rico. Seeing the projects in the background got her a little homesick. At least back home she would know who was really a popsicle salesman and who was only pretending to be. She felt out of bounds there.

Avery came over and kissed her on the forehead. "Hey there, pretty lady. I heard you got into a little dispute earlier today. Tell me what happened." He took off his shirt and pulled the belt from his pants.

She lowered her head. "I thought the Spanish dude downstairs was a popsicle man like we got back home, but it turned out he was everything but that."

He took off the bulletproof vest and threw it on the bed beside her, then set the big gun on the side table. "I guess that's more my fault than anything else. I should have warned you there is a lot of shysters out here, and you have to be very careful of who you're talking to. Lucky for you, King has us under surveillance." He looked down at the bags of money at the foot of the bed. "Did you go through my shit?"

She perked up and nodded. "Boy, I'm from the Stateway Projects, you know damn well I'm nosey. I peeped what you got in there, but I didn't touch nothing." She crossed her heart with a finger.

He kicked the bags under the bed. "Oh, I believe you. I don't take you as one of those thieving type. You got your shit together for the most part, and that's what draws me to you."

"Aw, I'm flattered," Tiny said, blushing. "I'm glad you can see that in me." She wrapped her arms around his midsection, loving the way his stomach muscles felt against her cheek.

"I do. I wouldn't have brought you down here if I didn't. Did you eat anything?" he asked, picking up the phone.

She shook her head. "Nall, I was waiting on you. I thought you would have been back way sooner." She squeezed him tighter and inhaled his cologne. The scent of him was turning her sexual senses on.

"Yeah, that's my bad, too. I didn't think business would take that long, but the good news is after I drop this money off, we'll be able to enjoy our vacation together. For now I'm gon' order us a little room service to put something in your stomach. We'll get a good night's rest, and tomorrow we'll enjoy ourselves. What do you think about that?"

She ran her hand across his stomach, turned her head sideways, and kissed it. "That sound good. You order what you gon' order, and I'm gon' snack on my appetizer right now." She unbuckled his pants and reached into his boxer shorts.

Chapter 14

She was awakened early in the morning by the sounds of church bells. At first she thought the bells were going off inside of their room. She had to shake her head to snap out of the daze. She ran her hand across the side of the bed, searching for Avery, only to find his portion empty. She sat up and looked around, blocking her face from the sunlight that shone through the big bay window. Slipping out of bed, the first thing she did was look under it in search of the duffle bags. They were missing, so she figured he was taking care of the last bit of business.

She showered, used the bathroom, did her hair, and was in the process of getting dressed when he came into the room, smiling. He was dressed in a suit like an average businessman. She found that ironic, but he did look handsome, nonetheless.

"Hey there, baby, I see you're up, looking like God's blessing to Chicago. That's good, too, 'cause we got a big day ahead. My man's shooting this new video with Jay and em' outta New York, then after that he gon' be having a yacht party, and you already know King got us R.S.V.P.'d. After that, I thought we'd come back here and burn the sheets up and plan what we gon' do the next day."

It took every ounce of sophistication Tiny had to not start jumping up and down. She was so excited. She barely knew what a yacht was, but she knew Jay was going to be there, and that's all that mattered. Plus, she had always wanted to be in a video or see one being made. She figured she would have to change her clothes and put on something a little more expensive and fashionable. There were bound to be a bunch of pretty girls there, so clothes would be the only way she could set herself aside from all the rest.

"Girl, did you hear what I said?"

She shook her head hard. "Huh?"

"You tripping."

"Nall, baby, I heard what you said. I was just going over in my head what I was about to pull out to wear." She reached down and plopped her suitcase on the bed.

"Don't worry about none of that. I'm about to take you shopping, anyway. We about to get flyer than the rest of them." He walked into the bathroom. "I'm about to hit this water, and when I come out, we out of here."

***

They were flying around Puerto Rico in a helicopter with so many shopping bags it was like they robbed the mall. If anyone told Tiny this would ever happen to her, she would have laughed in their face. People from the projects never dreamed that big. They only saw what was right in front of them, and that usually entailed death and destruction. This was the beautiful side of life, a side she thought only existed in the movies.

She straightened up the headphone-like things on her ears, praying they didn't mess up her hairdo as she looked out of the chopper down at the beautiful scenery. They passed over the governor's mansion, which was a very important landmark in Puerto Rico. They flew over El Morro, past the plazas, fountains, and the tropical forest.

She and Avery spent time walking through the Rio Camuy, and he dropped down to a squat and feasted on her goodies with her sundress pulled over his head inside the cave park while wild birds flew in and out of it, squawking and chirping.

To her, the old city was as beautiful as advertised. Everywhere they went, people offered them rum. Avery told her that in Puerto Rico almost everybody grew up drinking rum. She tasted it for the first time and didn't find it half bad. It wasn't something she would drink on a regular basis, but it wasn't bad.

They went to a festival where dancers put on a show for them while they beat on their drums and twirled their fire sticks. The women shook their hips so hard Tiny thought she would lose Avery to one of them. She had to keep stepping in front of him and kissing his lips so he didn't forget who he was there with.

There were so many pretty women and men there that Tiny felt she could stay there forever. The children were so nice and welcoming. The food was to die for, and she loved their customs. The city was rich with culture. Being there made her want to visit Africa. She felt before she got too old, she wanted to see her motherland.

"You know what? If you want to, we can plan a trip over there in a few months. I always wanted to see Africa, and I'd love to have the most beautiful black woman on my arm when I went." He looked down on her to see if his compliment hit home.

Tiny wrapped her arms around his narrow waist as the drummers in front of them danced a jig and twirled fire at the same time the females behind them shook their asses and flipped their long curly hair over their faces, looking back at the audience.

Tiny pointed to one of the women who was beyond gorgeous. "I wish we could take her back to the hotel with us. She's unbelievably gorgeous." Tiny licked her lips at the girl and she smiled. "Damn, she's hot."

"Who are you talking about?"

Tiny pointed directly at the attractive dancer and bit into her bottom lip.

Avery followed her gaze and rubbed his chin. "That's who you want to join us right there?"

Tiny shook her head. "Who said anything about joining us?" She smiled wickedly. "I was thinking about having her all to myself," she said, looking the woman up and down seductively.

Avery jerked his head back as if he were offended, then shrugged his shoulders. He walked out into the parade and grabbed her by the hand, bringing her into the audience where Tiny awaited, looking embarrassed.

"Tiny, this is Mya. Mya, this is Tiny, and she like what she sees. She thinks you and her would have an incredible time together. Now, what you think about that?"

The girl flipped her long hair out of her face and over her shoulders. There was a light dew of sweat on her forehead that made her look even more sexy.

She popped back on her legs, placing both

hands on her back, holding her waist, then looked up at Tiny like an innocent child. "Is that right? Do you really like me?" she asked in broken English.

Tiny blushed. She was so embarrassed she didn't know what to do. She felt like a little boy with a schoolhouse crush. She looked the girl up and down, then turned her head to the side and laughed. "Yeah, that's true. Out of all those dancers out there, I couldn't focus in on nobody but you."

Mya smiled and looked away. "That makes me feel good. I am used to men trying to hit on me, never a woman, but there is something about you that drives me wild. I would like to get to know you. When do you leave the island?"

Behind them, the parade continued to carry on. There was now a whole group of about 50 girls dancing to a slow reggae beat. Tiny wondered if the whole island was full of pure and naturally beautiful women. If that was the case, she hoped they stayed across the water and never came to Chicago, because if they did, they'd for sure snatch up all the men. With their thick frames and real hair, the sistas wouldn't have a chance. They were already losing out to the white girls. If they added the island Puerto Ricans to the mix, they didn't stand a chance. "I'll be here a few more days. Why, what do you have in mind?"

Mya ran her tongue across her lips. "I was hoping that before you left we could spend some time together." She turned to Avery, "King's cousin, do you think it can be arranged?"

He picked up one of her hands and made her turn around in a circle, marveling at her perfect body that was no doubt built as a playground for sex. The fact she was slightly bowlegged made things that much more hot.

"I can most definitely make that happen, just as long as y'all don't leave me in the lurches." He looked over to Tiny.

She walked up to him and kissed him on the lips. "That would never happen."

Mya leaned in and kissed Tiny on the cheek. "Alright then. I'll see you two soon."

**

Tiny was squeezing into her tight, low-cut Roberto Cavalli dress. The colors were all black with a spit of red, and she figured she'd complete the ensemble with off-setting, all-red Manolos with a three-inch lift. The heels were a bit uncomfortable, but it was the price she had to pay to look good, and good is definitely what she looked.

She'd gotten her hair re-braided by a woman on the beach who had twisted her hair so good she felt like traveling back to the island every time she'd need it done in the future. She'd had matching micro sea shells sewn in. Her body was freshly waxed and smooth as the day she came into the world. She'd even allowed the woman to shave her bald below the belt, so every time she took a step it felt as if she were traveling on an erotic journey.

Avery stepped into the room wearing an Armani tux, also all black, with a red vest and matching handkerchief. His Alexander McQueen Gators completed his ensemble, and his waves were so deep now that she could surf on them. Tiny thought he looked too fine. His black skin popped, and she felt like ripping his clothes off and sweating out her braids.

"Damn, baby, you sure are looking good. You sure I ain't gon' have to worry about you being snatched up tonight by one of them island girls?" She stepped on her tippy-toes and sucked on his lips. Though the comment seemed as if it were a joke, she was actually concerned.

He smiled slightly, nudging her to the side so he could look into the mirror. "Hey, what happens on the island stays on the island, am I right?"

"What? Boy, nall, you not right. I'm sitting here, serious. I don't want to have to kick one of them li'l curly-haired girl's asses for brushing all up on my man at this party. I'm serious, I'll bring the Stateways all through that muthafucka. We'll come back and burn this island down. Chicago, stand up!" she yelled, holding her hand over her mouth like a funnel.

Avery couldn't help laughing at her. He wrapped his arms around his stomach, bellowing with tears in his eyes. "Girl, you silly as hell. You already know I ain't 'bout to tick off my queen. I'm gon' do me, but you best believe I'm gon' give you that respect, 'cause at the end of the day it's all about us."

She smirked. "Yeah, uh-huh, that's what it better be about. I'mma hold you to that. Ooh, I want you to feel something." She grabbed his hand and put it under her dress, pulling her Victoria's Secret panties to the side. "You feel that?"

Avery ran his fingers over her thick sex lips, bald as an eagle. "Yo, you shaved the kitchen? Aw, shit, baby, you gotta let me get a sample of that right now." He slid his finger into her all the way to the second knuckle.

Her warmth enveloped him. Tangy juices clung to his fingers. Her walls vibrated against his digit. She moaned deep with her hot breath grazing his cheek.

She reached down and pulled his finger out of her. "That's what you got to look forward to tonight if you behave and don't make momma too mad."

"Yo, and we role playing?" He rubbed his hands together.

"Bet!"

***

To say Tiny was mesmerized would have been an understatement. She looked out of the chopper, giddy as a bum that had just won the lottery. She was so anxious to land that she felt like jumping out of the helicopter wearing a parachute just so the night of festivities could begin already.

They were in the air for only a few minutes when she spotted the huge yacht. It looked more like a ship to her, all white with the words "The Dynasty" painted on the side of it in big, bold letters. From as far as she could see, it was already full of people. There were numerous helicopters circling around the boat. They landed and emptied their patrons, and again ascended into the air, making way for the next chopper to do the same.

Tiny and Avery's helicopter had to make two full revolutions before they were able to land and exit. They stepped off and onto the yacht, greeted by female security, heavily armed and unnaturally beautiful. Tiny slid her arm into Avery's as they were cleared to enter what Tiny could have never had the imagination to have dreamed of.

All of the people she was accustomed to seeing on television from the hip hop world were there, and they had showed up to show out. From what she could tell, it was nothing more than a fashion show, and considering herself a young fashionista, as each woman walked past her she revealed what they were wearing in her own head.

The women were absolutely gorgeous, adorned in their foxes and furs. Dior, Chanel, Vera Wang, Givenchy, M.A.C. and even Gucci and Prada clung to the freshly-waxed and moisturized skins. Some of the women had their noses so far up in the air she could see all the way to their brains. They gave her a look that said they were better than her, and she didn't belong. They looked her up and down and turned up their noses, and then wrote her off. They paid special attention to Avery, though. After giving him a once-over, they smiled, and most kissed him on the cheek and left before he could introduce the dame on his arm. Tiny felt a little hurt and even more insecure than she had ever before.

The men, on the other hand, were handsome and gave her so much eye contact she felt violated. Every time Avery introduced her to someone, they would hug her and run their hands over her butt, cupping it. The first time it happened, she jumped and was ready to smack the record producer, but Avery gave her a look that said *just roll with it*. She also noticed every time he hugged a woman, he did the same thing to their asses, so Tiny thought it was something the upper crust did. It was like how Europeans kissed each other on both cheeks. The place was extremely elegant, posh, with crystal chandeliers and a huge ballroom with shiny floors, and waiters that served them in tuxedos and big bowties.

Mary J performed live on stage as they entered what resembled a small lounge in the lower portion of the huge yacht. There they slid into a booth as a bottle of Moet was placed on the table on top of a bucket of ice.

Avery scooted closer to her and wrapped his arm around her shoulder. "Baby, you're okay. You look a little uncomfortable." He said this and then kissed her on the neck, biting into it. She leaned closer to him to feel his teeth nearly piercing her skin.

She loved when he gave her displays of affection out of the blue, especially in an atmosphere where everyone was so classy and on a higher level than she was. She felt extremely insecure at the moment. She felt like running and hiding under a rock. "Wow, is it that obvious?" she asked, trying to smile.

He hugged her closer and sucked loudly on her neck. "Baby, it's good. Don't trip, 'cause ain't none of these bitches here got shit on you. Most of these broads plastic, and are so unhappy they cry themselves to sleep at night, and the other half got some kind of drug problem that's eating away at them. Ain't none of their men faithful, and most of these chicks you ain't even gon' see at the next party because they gon' be replaced. Trust that I know what I'm talking about."

She hoped he did keep talking, because he was making her feel a whole lot better. They said misery loves company, and she couldn't deny that hearing most of the females there were miserable did make her feel better about her place there, and herself. It was nice to know the 'haves' were as miserable as the 'have nots.' But then she got to thinking, what was the point if one always wound up in a state of unhappiness.

"I don't know, babe. I'm good, though. As long as I'm here with you, that's all that matters to me."

She laid her head on his shoulder.

"Avery? Avery is that you?"

Tiny looked up and saw one of her R&B idols. She couldn't believe she was sitting in front of her. She knew all of her songs by heart, and had just copped her latest CD. She wanted to know how Avery knew her, and if he could possibly get tickets to her next show when she came through Chicago.

Avery looked up and slid his arm from around Tiny's shoulders. "Yo, Monica, what's good, ma? Long time, no see," he said, standing up to hug her. He got his arms halfway around her when she pushed him slightly in the chest, preventing him from doing so.

"Boy, please. It's 'long time, no see' because of you. And who might this be?" she asked as if she were copping an attitude.

Now Tiny was starting to feel some type of way. It seemed to her they were more than friends. She could tell by Avery's uncomfortable body language. He started to stutter as if he had forgotten her name.

Tiny held out her hand. "My name is Zivial, and this is just my good friend, nothing more. It's a pleasure to meet you. You have an amazing voice."

Monica left her hand in the air and rolled her eyes. She turned to Avery. "So, you're bringing groupies on board now? I thought we were supposed to leave them backstage, or in the dressing room." She looked Tiny up and down and rolled her eyes again.

Avery stepped in front of her. "Yo', be cool, Monica. She cool. This my heart right here, and you gon' respect her or keep it moving."

Tiny felt her heart skip a beat. She couldn't believe he was standing up for her. She almost melted onto the floor. She fell in love with him in that moment.

"Are you serious? Do you know who you're talking to? You're going to choose her?" She turned to Tiny. "May I ask you what you're famous for?"

By this time Tiny had enough of playing coy. She felt that Chicago heat throbbing in her veins. She didn't care who Monica was or who she thought she was. In that moment she was just a regular female who was overstepping her bounds.

Tiny picked up her drink and threw it into her face. "Bitch, I'm famous for doing that."

Monica stood, looking appalled. Her hair matted to her face, her designer gown ruined. She wiped the champagne away and was about to run at Tiny when Avery raised his hand and the security guards shot to their table in blazing speed.

"Is there a problem?" the pretty guard asked with a face curled into a snarl.

"Yeah, we got one to go."

The guard immediately reached for Tiny, then Avery blocked her path. "Not her. I'm talking about this bitch right here. Get this stalker away from me."

Before Monica could protest, she was led away from their table.

Tiny kissed him on the cheek. "Baby, I hate to be a sore sport, but can we just get out of here?"

He looked shocked. "What, and let this bitch ruin our night? Absolutely not. Come on, let's dance." He pulled her onto the dance floor, and on stage Alicia began serenading the crowd. Avery wrapped his arms around her, and they danced close with her head on his shoulder.

She felt like the world had disappeared, and the only two who were left were the two of them.

***

Afterward, they took their champagne to the deck and hob knobbed with a few heavy hitters. That night Tiny met a lot of famous people, but none of them mattered to her. All she saw was Avery. She watched him wherever he went. Her eyes followed him around the room, and she started to hate when other females hugged him.

They were on the way to calling their chopper when someone tapped her on the shoulder. She turned around and came face-to-face with a short Spanish man.

"Say, mami, I wanna shoot you in my next video. We shooting it tomorrow on this yacht. I'mma have my chopper scoop you from El Sazon at 7:00 in the morning. You be there and you're booked." He looked her up and down. She felt as if she were naked the way he visually devoured her.

"I'm sorry, who are you?"

"Who am I? You gotta be joking, right? Who am I? I'm the one who produced him."

She looked over her shoulder and saw Jay walking across the deck with two women under his arms. She bugged her eyes out, turning star struck all over again.

"Yo, Jay, what it is?" the man said, giving him half a hug and a pound.

"Yo, you know, I can't complain." He looked Tiny up and down and smiled.

"I'm glad you like, because tomorrow she gon' be video vixen number two."

"What happened to Cassidy?"

The man dragged a finger across his neck. "She's out, and she's in. Besides, you two look beautiful together. How about it?"

Jay shrugged. "Yo, you make it happen. I'll bring the swagger, you bring the ladies."

Tiny felt lost. They were talking around her as if she didn't even exist. She had not given the man an answer, and yet he had already put her into the video. She felt a little bit uneasy. The women up under Jay's arms were giving her the nastiest of looks.

"So, how about it, mamita?"

She didn't know what to say. "I don't know. Um."

He cut her off. "It pays five thousand, and you'll work no more than four hours. On top of that, this video is going to be seen all around the world. It's going to be huge, and your pretty face is going to get a lot of camera time."

Tiny was speechless. All she could do was nod her head.

Chapter 15

By the second hour, Tiny started to respect every female she had ever seen in a video. She was put through so many trials she almost quit in the middle of the shoot. Every few seconds somebody was walking up to her and pulling her bikini further up and into her booty. Then they were reaching inside her top and rearranging her breasts. They talked to her as if she was trash, and the other girls never spoke a word to her. All they did was stay off in their corner until it was time to start rolling again.

At the duration of the shoot, they loaded them up into the helicopter and got mad when Tiny asked about her check. They gave her the run-around until finally Jay's PR rep said she would mail it to her.

She made it back to her room just after dark. Avery was laid out on the bed in his boxers, snoring like a mad man. She walked over to him and slapped his thigh. He jerked upward, slid his hand under the pillow, and came out with a big 9 millimeter. Tiny jumped back and threw her hands into the air.

"Hey, boy, watch where you're pointing that thing."

He wiped the fog out of his eyes and shook his head. "Damn, baby, why you sneaking up on me and shit. You know how paranoid I get." He sat up and grabbed her to his body. "What's good, though?"

She lowered her head and the tears started to flow. "They just took advantage of me at that shoot. They had me doing all that shit and didn't pay me nothing. Jay's rep said she was going to send me a check, but didn't even take down my information. I feel so stupid."

Avery jumped up and got on the phone. "I knew that punk-ass nigga was gon' try that shit. They always doing that shit, but not to my woman. I ain't with that fuck shit!" He started to put on his pants with one hand. "Yeah, this Avery. Stop that nigga Jay from leaving. I'll be over there in 10 minutes. A'ight, bet those." He snapped his vest on and threw a shirt over it.

Tiny tried to pull him. "Wait, where are you going, baby? It's not that serious, baby. I'll be okay, please," she whimpered.

He jerked away from her. "Tiny, fuck that, because that nigga asked me if he could use you in his video, and I gave him the nod and told him to pay you upfront. That punk deliberately defied me on some disrespectful shit. I don't like them New York niggas, anyway. They think they better than us, and they act like Chicago won't bring that noise on they ass. I'm about to make an example out this nigga." He curled up his lip and screwed a silencer onto the nozzle of his gun.

"You not about to kill him, are you?" She was starting to get worried. She liked what they had going and didn't want anything to get in the way of that. She wracked her brain to think of anything she could possibly say to make him change his mind, but she couldn't think of anything.

"Baby, can't we just leave? I swear I don't want that money. You're way more important than money. Please, listen to me."

The last thing she saw was his back as he left and slammed the door.

***

She stayed up worried about him all night. She felt sick to the stomach just thinking about what could have been taking place on her account. She didn't know what to do, so she started drinking and praying it would calm her nerves. When the clock hit 2:00 a.m. and he had not returned, she started guzzling way more than she should have. She didn't know how it happened, but she drifted off to sleep imagining him killing Jay.

She was pulled out of bed some time later by Avery. He told her to get up and to get dressed, that they were leaving the island prematurely because he had to see to some major new developments in Chicago. He tossed her a roll of money and continued packing his suitcase. "That's $10,000, and Jay sends his apologies."

She didn't ask questions, simply thanked him and packed her suitcases as well. As happy as she was to be on the island, she was even happier now that they were leaving it. She'd missed her home. She couldn't wait to see the windy city, to see the place she'd called home her entire life. She felt like she had missed out on so much.

The first thing she would do would be to visit Ariana. She wanted to pick her up and to hold her close to her heart. She wanted to kiss her forehead and let her know everything was going to be okay, that she'd always have her back, no matter what.

As they flew back home, all she could think about was the little girl. Visions of her fighting for her life in the hospital. She thought of Amber and felt even more sad. What a waste of a life. How could a person deprive their child of their presence on purpose? That was something Tiny didn't think she would ever be able to understand.

Avery was very quiet on the flight back. He looked out the window in deep thought. He'd shake his head for a few seconds, and then mumble slightly under his breath.

She laid her head onto his shoulder. "Baby, are you okay?"

"Yeah, I'm good. Why you ask me that?"

"I'm just checking on my man, that's all. I see you over here talking to yourself, and I just figured you had something on your mind." She looked up to him.

He leaned down and kissed her on the forehead. "Yeah, I do. Baby, when I get back here, I gotta take care of a bunch of business for King, so I might be busy for a few days. Since I been gone, some foul shit went down with one of the men I brought into the fold. King didn't tell exactly what that was, but all I know is I gotta answer for him because I swore by this dude, and that makes me accountable for his actions."

"What is he, a baby or something? Why should you be held accountable for another grown man? That doesn't make sense to me. We have enough of our own problems."

He sat up in his chair and lit a blunt. "I know, but that's how the game goes. Before I could be put down, somebody had to swear by me, too, so if I fucked up, their head would be on the chopping block." He took a deep pull and blew the smoke out in a thick cloud.

Tiny squirted some lotion into her hand and rubbed it into her arms. "I thought you said King was your cousin?"

Avery nodded. "He is, but when it comes to the game, that don't mean shit. Money is thicker than blood."

Tiny's stomach turned. She had heard how dangerous King and his organization was. They were relentless. They killed at the drop of a hat with no mercy. This made her worry about the welfare of Avery.

"Baby, do you think you'll be able to squash things? Are you going to be okay?"

***

Tiny got her answer three weeks after their vacation was over. Everything was going so smoothly. She'd gotten right back into the groove of things at the salon. At the technical college, things were going just as well. She'd visited Ariana four times, and each time she saw her, she appeared to be getting stronger and stronger.

She'd heard through the grapevine Jaheim had been arrested for petty theft, which meant he'd be back out in no time, but that didn't concern her. She wanted to bump into him so she could convince him to sign over his parental rights to her. She'd made up her mind that she wanted to raise Ariana as her own child, and she didn't see why Jaheim would deny her that right. He seemed as if he didn't want anything to do with the baby.

Her relationship with Avery was almost indescribable. He was a great man to her, very respectful and considerate. He treated her like a queen, and told her everything that was on his mind. Some nights she sat up and listened to him and was almost scared to tears.

He confided in her often of his fear of King and the organization, because they were full of cutthroats. None of them felt compassion for the other, and everything revolved around money and King's word. Chris was King's right-hand man, and he was all over the place. He was pimping, running a chain of strip clubs, heavy in the sale of guns, and on top of that he was the overseer of the workers who pounded the pavement to keep the heroin flowing throughout the city. It was also rumored he was using the product. In King's eyes, Chris could do no wrong. He was golden, and King took everything Chris said at face value. The only bad thing about that was Chris hated Avery. He looked at him as a threat, as a replacement because he was so good of a worker. He had a way of getting people to follow him, and those that did respected him so much they never thought about crossing him. They looked up to him and genuinely trusted him to have their best interest at hand.

Chris disliked this. He hated hearing Avery's name as much as he did. He didn't like the way all of the pavement pounders looked up to him as if he were some kind of god. He and King had built up their organization from the ground, and Chris felt there was no way he would allow Avery to slip in to get a slot. The cousin thing bothered him immensely.

Night after night, Avery would relay his feelings to Tiny, and she would sit up and listen to him, not knowing what to say or do. She felt he didn't want her to talk, all he wanted her to do was listen, so she gave him that shoulder he needed.

It was a muggy night, too hot to be outside, so they had chosen to stay indoors the entire day with the exception of a few runs Avery made in the name of business. They snuggled together in the bed and watched movie after movie, eating slices of pizza and potato chips. To Tiny it felt magical. She loved spending time with him. She loved watching him lie around with his shirt off. Being held in his arms made her feel like a little girl. Things were going great. The only thing that bothered her a tad bit was the fact she had missed her period the last couple weeks. She was afraid to take a pregnancy test, and she was afraid to tell him she had missed her period. Things were going so good that she did not want to jeopardize anything.

Then it happened, the same night they had chosen to stay in. They were in the bedroom, in the midst of making sweet, passionate love, the kind that's rough and intimate, getting fully in tune with each other's senses, when their bedroom door was kicked open. Ten masked men in all black surrounded the bed and smacked Avery on the back of the head with the handle of a gun, knocking him out. He fell on top of her and was dragged from her body. Then she was snatched up and forced into a chair. They tied her arms behind her and her legs to each other. She felt a blow to the back of her head and everything faded to black.

***

When she came to, a caramel-skinned man in a bulletproof vest was holding something under her nose that smacked her senses and made her want to run. She tried to move, but couldn't. Her hands and legs were bound. The corner of her mouth felt sore. She looked to her right and saw Avery sat next to her, also bound and gagged. The both of them were naked as jaybirds.

The caramel-skinned man walked over to Avery and held the same thing under his nose that had jarred her awake. Avery slowly came to. When he regained his senses, he tore his head away from the man's hand.

Tiny didn't know where they were, but they were no longer at her condo. They were in some kind of a basement – a grungy basement. She'd seen more than four rats skitter across the floor already. She became scared and wondered what the men wanted with them.

The caramel-skinned man was the only one without a mask. Inside the room were at least 15 other people, masked and heavily armed. All Tiny could see were the pupils of their eyes.

The caramel-skinned man walked over to Avery, took the gag out of his mouth and knelt down.

Avery smacked his lips together before finding his voice. "What the fuck is going on, Chris? Why am I and my lady down here?" he asked through a dry, raspy voice.

Chris laughed. "Well, ain't it obvious?" He stood up and ran his hand through the air. "You already know what it means when you show up down here on the receiving end. It means you done fucked up, nigga! So tell me, Avery, what have you did to fuck up?"

Avery struggled against his bonds. "Man, I ain't did shit, and you know it. You just fucking with me because you can. I ain't never did nothing to you, Chris, but try to have your back. I don't get why you doing this shit."

Chris took a cigar out of the inner pocket of his suit jacket and lit it. He blew the smoke straight into the air. "Wow, those are some strong words there, brother. You sure you don't want to take none of that back? I mean, at least for your woman's sake over here?" Chris walked over to Tiny and put his hand on her shoulder. He reached down and snatched the gag out of her mouth. "What's your name, little sister?"

She smacked her lips together and tried to swallow her spit because her mouth was so dry. "My name is Tiny, and I haven't done anything to you, so why am I here?"

Chris inhaled the smoke into his lungs and blew it into her face. "Avery, I have to admit, this little lady right here is fine as a muthafucka. I don't know where you found her at, but lucky you. It's a shame we gon' have to take her off this earth."

Tiny started crying as soon as she heard those words. She knew the man was serious. She saw her life flash before her eyes. She thought about her mother, her father, Ariana, and her favorite Aunty Gwen whom she had not visited in a while. She missed her so much and she promised herself if she made it out of this debacle, she would drive over to her home in Riverdale just to hug and kiss her.

"Chris, why are you doing this? What have I done to deserve this treatment?"

Chris spun on the balls of his feet and stopped directly in front of Avery. "You brought that thieving-ass nigga Red into the fold, and he done made off with $75,000, and now he can't be found! So, you tell me where he is, and where the money is, and I'll spare your lives. That don't mean I'm not fucking you up, though. You gon' feel this steel, that's law! But I will let you live."

Tiny closed her eyes. She knew they were dead meat. There was no way Avery knew where Red was. If he had known, he would have told her and he would have been prepared to face their impending onslaught. She could tell he was completely caught off guard, and that worried her.

"Chris, you know I would never cross King, man. That's my blood. I don't know what's going on with Red, but whatever he did, I ain't have no knowledge of it. I have cleaned up after him before. I can't keep doing that shit, bro. I got my own life to think about."

Chris walked up to him and stubbed the blunt out on his neck. Avery screamed at the top of his lungs and Tiny started crying. She could smell the mixture of weed and skin floating through the air.

"Nigga, all I'm hearing you say is you don't know where our money is, which means you have to be chastised. That's 75 thousand dollars. That's a whole lot of money. I have to go in front of King and explain how I fucked up by putting y'all into position to handle that load. Do you understand me?" Chris lit the blunt again and blew the smoke toward the ceiling. "So, tell me, Avery, what am I supposed to do about this loss? And be careful, because the next time I put out this blunt it's gon' be on your li'l girlfriend over here."

The hole in his neck still had smoke coming from it. "Chris, I don't know what you want me to say. I don't get down like that. I would never cross y'all. I got about 15 thousand put up of my own money, and I can do what I gotta do to get the rest, but I swear to you I'm innocent."

Chris grabbed Tiny by the hair, pulled her head backward, and stubbed the blunt out in the same spot he had put it out on Avery's neck. She screamed at the top of her lungs. The pain was so excruciating she shot up from the seat and wound up falling onto her side on the floor.

Chris laughed. "Well, damn, one thing we know for sure is baby girl ain't no masochist."

Avery tried to break his bonds. "Come on, Chris, man, that shit ain't funny. She didn't do nothing to you, and she ain't got nothing to do with this. You know King don't be condoning us hurting women. You're real foul right now, bro, for real."

Chris walked up to him and backhanded him across the face. "Nigga, fuck what you talking about, and fuck that bitch! King don't condone niggaz stealing from his organization, either. Now, you tell me what you gon' do about this money, or I'm about to leave both of y'all stanking and then throw you in that incinerator over there."

Tiny struggled to sit up, the pain in her neck unbearable. "I can get the money."

Chris stepped over to her form. "What did you just say?"

She flinched, thinking he was about to strike her. "Please, Chris, I can get the money. Just don't hurt us anymore, please."

Chris squinted his eyes. "Damn, my bad, shorty." He reached down and pulled her up and back into the seat. "Now, how are you going to get this money?"

"Look, I'll need a couple of days, but no more than three, and I promise you I'll have the remaining 60 thousand. We can add that to his 15 thousand, and that will give you 75 on the head. Will that be cool?"

Chris turned to look at Avery. "Wait a minute, that 15 thousand is already cashed in. Avery, you gon' pay that just for taking us through all of this. So, it's either your girl gon' have to come up with the whole 75, or I'm gon' have to kill you, bro. And trust me, it will be my pleasure."

Tiny spoke up. "Wait a minute, you can't kill him."

Chris turned and gave her a look as if she'd just insulted him. "And why the fuck not?"

"Because I'm pregnant with his baby."

Avery perked up, and then slumped his head.

"Fuck, man!"

Chris jerked his shoulders. "Congratulations. So, this is how this is going to go. You're going to get 48 hours to bring me this money, at which point in time he's going to still be down here in this basement, waiting on you to come through. We gon' feed him one time, and that's it. He gon' go to the bathroom on his self, and he ain't leaving from that chair until you get back here. I ain't worried about you calling the cops because we own all of them in this city. By the time they make it here, we would have been tipped off five times, and he will have been dead and gone."

"I'm not going to the cops."

Chris shrugged his shoulders. "I don't give a fuck if you do. I hope you do, that way I can kill this nigga. You got 48 hours to bring me that money. A second too late and this nigga's a dead man, and then we coming for you."

Tiny swallowed. "Okay."

Chris saw a rat running across the floor and reached down and caught it. He held it down and went into his pocket, pulling out a Swiss Army knife. He cut its head off, causing blood to squirt up into the air. The rat squealed and its mouth continued to move even though its head was separated from its body. Chris took his lighter and ran it up and down the rodent, singeing its hairs. He did this for a few moments, and then threw it onto Avery's lap. "Here you go, nigga. This is your one and only meal."

T.J. & Jelissa

Chapter 16

Time was of the essence. Tiny pulled her truck up to the church after fixing her makeup in the mirror. She had to gather herself because she was freaking out. Her minute that ticked away was a minute Avery grew closer to death. She had the weight of the world on her shoulders and prayed to God they would not crumble.

She opened the doors to the church and slid into a pew as the pastor stood in front, giving his sermon about the end times. Those were times she did not want to think about. A superstitious part of her started to equate his sermon with her and Avery's pending demise. She thought it was ironic he would be preaching about death when they were so close to it being their reality.

She sat and listened impatiently, constantly looking at her watch as minute after minute ticked away. She shook one leg and bounced it up and down on her toes as she sat. She couldn't sit still.

As soon as he was done preaching and the church started to let out, she almost ran to the front of the church and pulled him to the side.

"I need to see you, and we need to talk right now," she said, already heading down toward his office.

He nodded. "I'll meet you down there in five minutes. Allow me to clear this sanctuary."

"Okay, but hurry." She walked away from him and directly into the path of Lisa. She tried to avoid the girl, but as she stepped to the right, Lisa did as well. Then she tried the left, and it happened again.

"Hey there, Zivial. Haven't heard from you in a while. What's new?"

"Lisa, look, I'm really in a hurry. I'm going through something right now, and I don't want to be rude." She went around her and down the stairs and waiting outside of the pastor's office. She looked at her watch again.

So far she had already lost three hours.

***

He stepped in and closed the door behind him. "Zivial, what's the problem?"

"Look, I don't know how much to tell you, or what to do, but I need a favor from you, and I don't want you to ask me a bunch of questions. I need for you to just trust me."

He loosened his tie and sat down behind his desk. He pointed to the chair in front of him. "Okay, why don't you have a seat and tell me what you need."

Tiny sat down for a few seconds and then bounced back up. "Now, I know this is going to sound crazy, but you have to know it is very important, and I would not come to you unless my back was against the wall." She paused and looked him over. He sat staring at her as if he were waiting for her to go on. "Harold, I need $70,000, and I need it by tomorrow morning, no later."

He stood up. "Are you out of your freaking mind? $70,000? Where am I going to get that kind of money?"

Tiny blinked tears. "Stop the bullshit, now.

Someone's life depends on it. I need this money by tomorrow or they're going to kill him, and then me. Please help me. I am begging you," she whimpered, trying not to break down altogether. She felt her knees going weak.

"Zivial, what are you talking about? Who's going to kill you, and how do you know? Should we go to the police?"

"No! There can't be any cops. If the cops are called, they'll know, and they will kill him. And then they're coming for me. Now, please, help me!" She broke down and fell to her knees, crying her eyes out. He ran from around the desk and wrapped his arms around her.

"Zivial, I'll do what I can. I don't know if I can get you 70 grand, but we'll go down and see what I can withdraw. In fact, I'll call right now. I have a secret account Mrs. Moore doesn't know about. It has about 50 grand inside of it. I also know she has one, as well, and I don't question her about it. I'll give you the 50 that's in there if you promise to never speak to me again. I mean, from now on we have no more dealings, and you don't blackmail me anymore. You destroy all of the evidence you have against me. Is that a deal?"

"But where will I get the other 20 grand?"

"I don't know, but I'm sure you'll figure it out."

He shocked her when he moved the small refrigerator to the side and bent down. There was a little rug there that he flipped backward. He removed two wooden pieces from the floorboard, and then Tiny saw his hand moving one way, and then the next as if he were turning a dial. It came to her in that moment that he was opening a safe. She saw the safe's metal door open, and he reached his arm in and began counting stacks and stacks of money. They lined up on the floor beside him. His lips quivered as he counted them to himself.

Tiny tried to rubberneck and look over his shoulder to see how much was exactly in the safe. She couldn't quite see from her vantage point. She took a step further and he seemed to move more to his left to block her view.

When he was sure he'd counted out fifty thousand, he slammed the safe shut and put everything back into place. Wrapping the bundles in his shirt, he stood and dropped them all on his desk. "Alright, here you go. This is $50,000. This concludes our business. I don't know what you've gotten yourself into, but I don't want any part of it. This is all I have for you, and I encourage you to also hold up your end of the deal."

Tiny knew there was more money in that safe. It would take the pastor only a few weeks to get it all back. Every Sunday the fold poured in from their homes and gave his church gracious donations of hefty sums. He had way more than $70,000, she was sure of it.

"Pastor, thank you," she said, tossing the bundles into her big handbag. "I really appreciate you coming through for me, you have no idea what kind of a bind I am in." She zipped up the bag and glanced down at the floor.

The pastor walked toward the door, getting ready to open it and let her out. He wanted to be rid of the girl. He didn't know what kind of trouble she was in, but he wanted no part of it. He wanted to move forward with his life. He had made a mistake, and surely God was punishing him as He had done David and Bathsheba. The Lord had blessed the pastor with as many fruits of the world he could have possibly ever wanted. He gave him a loyal wife and a beautiful family with well-disciplined and God-fearing children. He gave him a big house and two high-priced automobiles. He gave him a big congregation with loyal believers who gave him their all just to lead them beside still waters. He had been blessed a million times over, and how did he repay the Lord?

He repaid Him by lusting after young women and sleeping around on his wife. He spent the church's money to fund his side escapades. He had, in a sense, turned his back on God, and he felt that, in a sense, this was His way of making him see his wrongs and turn away from them. The money was nothing. It was the loss of his congregation that worried him. The dismantling of his foundations around him. He just wanted to be rid of the girl. He didn't know what happened to Amber, but he silently prayed she never resurfaced – her or the child Zivial once spoke of.

"Well, Zivial, you have a wonderful life. I wish you all the best. Please never come back here and never speak of me again."

Tiny made her way toward the door, but then stopped in her tracks. She was silent for a long while, and then she turned to him. "Harold, I'm sorry, but I need that other twenty grand. I have no other way of getting it. You have to understand I am in a bind here. Now, I know you have it in that safe right there, so please stop jerking me around. Time is of the essence."

She balanced her weight from one foot to the other, biting into her bottom lip nervously. She was in no position for him to deny her. She needed the money a lot more than he did. What else could he possibly need? He had everything a man could want or need. $70,000 was a bridge that stood between her and her man's life.

The pastor slammed the door. "What is the matter with you, little girl? Haven't you taken enough from me? Why is it you wish to be greedy? Do you not know you are now sinning against this church?"

Tiny had to stand back because he walked up on her and stood in her face. She could smell his hot breath. It smelled like coffee and a hint of spearmint gum. Beads of sweat poured down his face and ran into the collar of his tailor-made suit.

She took another step backward. "Pastor, you don't understand. I –"

He cut her off. "You're right that I don't understand, and I don't want to. I just gave you $50,000, and you're standing there ornery and indignant as if I haven't given you anything at all. How dare you come into this church in the first place and ask for such a sum? Your behavior is an abomination. You embarrass not only yourself, but your parents, as well, who raised you to be a young woman and not a beggar. Now, whatever situation you have gotten yourself into, I have helped you more than enough. This is not my fight any longer.

It's yours!"

When he hollered in her face, she almost lost her cool and punched him. His spit flew and caught her on the side of the mouth. She wiped it away with blazing speed, disgusted it almost went inside of her mouth.

"Hey, back up! That's not cool, man. I get it, you no longer want to help, but you better not forget I'm the one that covered up you getting a 16-year-old pregnant. I hid that corruption from the church, so don't try and make it seem like you're the only one that's helped out or gave a favor. If not for me, you wouldn't even have a church to have a safe in." She bumped him as she walked past him. "But I'll leave, and you don't have to worry about me ever again."

She twisted the knob on the door and nearly jumped out of her skin when Lisa fell into the office. "What the hell?"

She fell all the way to her knees, then looked up at the both of them with anger in her eyes. "What the hell is going on here?" She stood up, rubbing the spots on her knees where she had scraped them.

Tiny walked around her and shot out of the office. She took the stairs two at a time and ran out of the church. Sitting in her car, she tried to gather herself. Her chest rose and fell. She clutched the bag to her protectively, wiped her face, and picked up her phone.

Chris picked up on the second ring. "Yes, my dear? Do you have something for me?"

Tiny swallowed. "I have 50 of it right now. Can I bring that to you?"

"There is no need. Look across the street. Do you see that black-on-black Rolls Royce with the driver's window slightly cracked?"

Tiny looked in all directions, and finally across the street she spotted the car he spoke of. The window rolled all the way down and a woman stuck her arm out and waved. "Yeah, I see it. What do you want me to do?"

"Take the money over to the car and drop it in the window. If it's 50 thousand, you have 20 to go, and the clock's ticking." The line disconnected.

Tiny took a deep breath and was about to open her door when a big city bus rolled past, almost taking the driver's side door off with it. She slammed the door just in time, her heart beating so hard it felt like it was coming out of her chest.

She opened the door again and then ran across the street and dropped the bag into the window as directed. Glancing into the car, she could see it was fully-loaded with women who were heavily armed. They gave her a look as if to say they were following her, and wanted her to slip up so they could dead her. She swallowed before running back across the street.

She sat in the car for ten minutes before she found the strength to drive away, not knowing where she was going.

Chapter 17

She ran through the doors of the beauty salon and into a packed establishment. She heard the patrons calling her name, and even a few of the workers, but she paid them no mind. She kept walking until she got to the back of the shop where the door read "Owner." She knocked on it and got no answer. She knocked three more times, and it was the same result.

"Girl, she on vacation," Mary said as she whipped a girl's perm.

Tiny looked the heavyset woman up and down. "What did you say?" She felt her stomach drop.

Mary continued whipping the woman's hair. She was a big girl. She had on all red and looked like a big jug of Kool-Aid. "I said she gone, and has been for the last couple days. She went to the Caribbean and ain't supposed to be back until next week sometime."

Next week. Next week they would both be dead. They would be resting in peace, probably chopped up and thrown down an incinerator. *Why is this happening?* she thought. Her boss had been her last hope. She thought maybe she could get an advance and promise to pay her back, but now she was out of the country. She didn't know what she would do.

She ran back out of the salon and saw the Rolls Royce parked behind her car. She paused for a second, and then shook her head and got into her car and drove off. There was one other option.

***

Tiny ran upstairs to her apartment, grabbed the book bag full of evidence and then ran back down the stairwell. She peeled away from the curb, got out her cellphone, and called Mrs. Moore. She worked at an afterschool program that was fifteen blocks away from the church. She told the old woman she was on her way to meet her, and it was very important and a matter of life and death. She told her not to tell Harold she was on her way because it concerned him. The old woman told her to hurry.

When Tiny got there, the mothers had arrived to collect their children. They waited until the last child was picked up and Mrs. Moore closed the door to the community center and locked it. Tiny did not wait for any pleasantries. She walked over to a television that was connected to a built-in VCR. She knelt down and pulled out the first tape from her bag and popped it into the device.

Harold and Amber could be seen going at it in the most explicit form of sex. On screen, Harold was guiding his penis into her buttocks while she held her cheeks apart and begged him to ram it into her. He gripped her hair and pulled her neck backward and thrust into her while she hollered as if she were being killed.

Tiny looked back to see the facial expression of Mrs. Moore. She had her hands over her face in complete shock. Feeling she was onto something, she took that tape out and slid in another one where Amber was giving him oral sex and calling him daddy while he fingered her rosebud.

She was about to put in another tape when Mrs. Moore yelled out, "Enough! What is going on here?"

Tiny took the tape out and put it back into her bag. "That girl you see is only 16 years old, and the pastor, your husband, took advantage of her. That's statutory rape. I believed in him and his message, and he did this to my friend. I'm going to the cops."

She made her way toward the doors when Mrs. Moore blocked her path.

"Wait a minute, Zivial. We can talk about this, please."

"What's there to talk about? He raped her, and I am seeking justice."

She hoped her bluff was affecting her the way she needed it to. Time was of the essence. All she needed was the last twenty. She had to work the sister. She had to get that money out of her. She remembered the pastor saying the woman had a secret account. His words replayed themselves again and again in her head.

"Zivial, I've known you all of your life. I know your mother, and I know your father, all of your siblings. I have never tried to hurt you or your family. If you do this, if you go to the police, you're going to ruin my family, and you're going to have my husband taken away for a long time. He'd die in prison. Please don't do this. Don't hurt us this way." The woman fell to her knees, begging.

Tiny knew she had her right where she wanted her. She felt bad for going to the extremes she did, but she felt it was the only way. Two lives depended on it.

"Then what do you suggest I do, Mrs. Moore? This girl is pregnant and afraid to face her family. They left her in my care, which makes me responsible for her. This is a hell of a dilemma."

Mrs. Moore was in tears at this time. "I don't know, maybe I can give you some money to make this all go away. Please, just tell me how much it will take?"

Tiny looked to the sky and thanked the heavens. She felt she was about to succeed. "I need twenty thousand, and I need it right away."

Mrs. Moore nodded. "Done. And if I give you this money, you'll give me all the tapes."

"I will. You will have nothing to worry about, that is my word."

"Okay, I'm going to hold you to that. I'll have the money for you first thing Monday morning."

Tiny's eyes almost rolled out of her head. "Monday morning? Wait a minute, today is only Wednesday. I can't wait until Monday. I'll be dead before then." She turned to Mrs. Moore. "No, I need this money by tomorrow morning or we don't have a deal. I'm sorry, but I'll be forced to go to the cops."

Mrs. Moore became bewildered. "I have an account, a secret one, that I can tap. There is $19,600 in it. You can have every penny. I will bring it to you first thing in the morning when the bank opens. Can you wait until then?"

The missing $400 bothered Tiny, but it was as close as she could get, so she couldn't complain. "You cannot speak to your husband or anybody about this. You cannot go to the cops or even tell

224

Lisa. If you do, then all bets are off. Now, do I have your word?"

Mrs. Moore nodded.

***

Tiny didn't get any sleep that night. She didn't even try to. Every time she even blinked her eyes, she saw her own death, and Avery being tortured to death. She broke out into a bad sweat and started hyperventilating.

At 9:00 the next morning, Mrs. Moore came and dropped off the money. She handed over all the tapes with the exception of three. She didn't know if she would have to use them again, but she liked having the insurance.

As soon as she left, Tiny jumped onto her cellphone and called Chris. He told her he would be over personally to pick it up in a few hours. When Tiny inquired about Avery, she said she wanted to hear his voice. Avery mumbled on the phone, and she shouted into it that she loved him. Chris told her if all of the money was there, he'd let him go after a sound ass-whooping and they would be free. She hung up the phone.

She figured she would tell him about the missing 400 dollars when he got there.

As soon as Tiny hung up, there was a knock at her door, which was odd because usually the front desk announced when she had a visitor downstairs and she had to give them permission to let them up. She felt strange because the person was already at her door. She peeked through the peephole and saw a distraught Lisa. That was odd. She didn't feel like dealing with her at that moment, but she opened the door anyway. Lisa bumped her and walked right in.

Tiny closed the door behind her. "Excuse you, what are you doing here?"

Lisa paced back and forth, staring at the floor. "You scurvy bitch. How dare you?" she spat.

"Excuse me? What did you just say?" Tiny's heart dropped. This was the last thing she needed. Chris was on his way, and Lisa had to be gone long before he got there.

"How dare you blackmail my people? How dare you treat my father like that after he helped you and your whore friend? We both know that bitch is grown. How dare you make her out to be a senseless child?"

Tiny swallowed. "Look, Lisa, I don't know what you're talking about, but obviously you're mistaken. I think you should just leave. I'm expecting company, and I have to tidy up before they get here."

She walked to the door and opened it. Outside in the hallway, she could see her nosey neighbor Ms. Applebaum trying to look inside of her apartment. The old lady gave her a crazy look.

"There's a lot of noise coming from your place. You're disturbing my nap."

"I'm sorry, I'll try to keep it down."

"Don't try. Do it." She closed her door.

"You have to leave, Lisa, now. I'm not going to ask you again," she said.

Lisa ran up on her so fast she could not even react. "You fucking bitch! I'm not leaving until you give me back my parents' money." She stood all the way in Tiny's face. She was six inches taller than her, so her chin was against Tiny's forehead.

Tiny had enough. She was so sick of being bullied and everyone trying to take advantage of her. She didn't know what she was doing, but all of a sudden she pushed the girl so hard she flew backward, tripped, and landed on the glass table, shattering it. Tiny was amazed at her own strength. "Holy shit!"

Lisa must have been a trooper, because within seconds she stood up and rushed her at full speed, slamming her back into the door so hard it knocked the wind out of Tiny. She fell and sat on her ass against the door.

She looked up in time to see Lisa searching through her kitchen drawers. She slowly made it to her feet and mustered up enough strength to run into the kitchen and tackle her against the refrigerator. They both fell to the floor, and the knife Lisa had obtained from the drawer slid across the linoleum.

Tiny jumped on top of her and slapped her upside the face again and again until she bucked upward and flipped her off.

Lisa grabbed her long braids and slung Tiny against the wall by them. She crashed with a loud thud, and the girl jumped on top of her and punched her square in the nose, busting it. She yelled out in pain.

"Give me the money, you bitch, or I'm going to kill you!" She grabbed the knife off the floor and held it in the air.

There was a loud knocking at the door. They

could hear Ms. Applebaum yelling. Lisa looked up, and that gave Tiny a split second to jerk her head up, head-butting the girl. She fell backward, dazed, her nose bleeding. She started to crawl across the floor toward Tiny.

Tiny shot up, ready to run out of the apartment to escape, but then felt Lisa pull her by the collar, almost choking her. She jerked away with all of her might, freeing herself, and ran across the room toward the door with Lisa in hot pursuit.

She passed the living room table and pulled out a chair to create a diversion. Lisa must have been closer to her than she thought, because she heard the girl topple over and then scream.

She rushed and pulled the chain off of the door, and then paused and looked backward. Lisa lay on her face, not moving, a pool of blood slowly starting to form around her.

"Lisa? Lisa, stop playing," she said, slowly walking toward her.

The girl began to jerk. Tiny flipped her over and saw she had landed on the butcher's knife. It was stuck into her stomach. Not thinking, Tiny reached down and pulled it out of her. As soon as she did, blood started to spurt out in thick rivulets.

Ms. Applebaum pushed the door in. "What's going on in here? Oh, my God!"

Tiny turned around with the knife in her hand. "Ms. Applebaum, it's not what you think. I —"

The old lady turned around and fell, then shot into her own apartment and slammed the door, just as Tiny's cellphone began ringing.

In a state of pure shock, she answered it.

"I'm here. Bring my money down to me."

To be continued...
Loyal to the Game 2
Coming July 15th

Stay Connected with Us!

Text **LOCKDOWN** to 22828 to stay up-to-date with new releases, sneak peaks, contests and more...
Thank you!

Coming Soon from Lock Down Publications/Ca$h Presents

BOW DOWN TO MY GANGSTA

By **Ca$h & Jamaica**

TORN BETWEEN TWO

By **Coffee**

BLOOD OF A BOSS **IV**

By **Askari**

BRIDE OF A HUSTLA **III**

THE FETTI GIRLS

By **Destiny Skai**

WHEN A GOOD GIRL GOES BAD **II**

By **Adrienne**

LOVE & CHASIN' PAPER **II**

By **Qay Crockett**

THE HEART OF A GANGSTA **II**

By **Jerry Jackson**

TO DIE IN VAIN **II**

By **ASAD**

LOYAL TO THE GAME **II**

By **TJ & Jelissa**

A DOPEBOY'S PRAYER **II**

By **Eddie "Wolf" Lee**

A HUSTLER'S DECEIT **II**

THE BOSS MAN'S DAUGHTERS **III**

BAE BELONGS TO ME **II**

By **Aryanna**

A KINGPIN'S AMBITON

By **Ambitious**

<u>Available Now</u>

(CLICK TO PURCHASE)

<u>RESTRAINING ORDER **I & II**</u>

By **CA$H & Coffee**

<u>LOVE KNOWS NO BOUNDARIES **I II & III**</u>

By **Coffee**

<u>LAY IT DOWN **I & II**</u>

<u>LAST OF A DYING BREED</u>

By **Jamaica**

<u>PUSH IT TO THE LIMIT</u>

By **Bre' Hayes**

<u>BLOOD OF A BOSS **I II & III**</u>

By **Askari**

<u>THE STREETS BLEED MURDER **I, II & III**</u>

THE HEART OF A GANGSTA

By **Jerry Jackson**

CUM FOR ME

CUM FOR ME 2

CUM FOR ME 3

An **LDP Erotica Collaboration**

BRIDE OF A HUSTLA **I & II**

By **Destiny Skai**

WHEN A GOOD GIRL GOES BAD

By **Adrienne**

A GANGSTER'S REVENGE **I II III & IV**

THE BOSS MAN'S DAUGHTERS

THE BOSS MAN'S DAUGHTERS II

A SAVAGE LOVE **I & II**

BAE BELONGS TO ME

By **Aryanna**

A DOPEBOY'S PRAYER

By **Eddie "Wolf" Lee**

WHAT ABOUT US **I & II**

NEVER LOVE AGAIN

THUG ADDICTION

By **Kim Kaye**

THE KING CARTEL **I, II & III**
By **Frank Gresham**
THESE NIGGAS AIN'T LOYAL **I, II & III**
By **Nikki Tee**
GANGSTA SHYT **I II &III**
By **CATO**
THE ULTIMATE BETRAYAL
By **Phoenix**
DON'T FU#K WITH MY HEART **I & II**
By **Linnea**
BOSS'N UP **I & II**
By **Royal Nicole**
I LOVE YOU TO DEATH
By Destiny J
I RIDE FOR MY HITTA
I STILL RIDE FOR MY HITTA
By **Misty Holt**
LOVE & CHASIN' PAPER
By **Qay Crockett**
TO DIE IN VAIN
By **ASAD**

BOOKS BY LDP'S CEO, CA$H
(CLICK TO PURCHASE)

TRUST IN NO MAN

TRUST IN NO MAN 2

TRUST IN NO MAN 3

BONDED BY BLOOD

SHORTY GOT A THUG

THUGS CRY

THUGS CRY 2

THUGS CRY 3

TRUST NO BITCH

TRUST NO BITCH 2

TRUST NO BITCH 3

TIL MY CASKET DROPS

RESTRAINING ORDER

RESTRAINING ORDER 2

IN LOVE WITH A CONVICT

Coming Soon

BONDED BY BLOOD 2

BOW DOWN TO MY GANGSTA

T.J. & Jelissa

www.ingramcontent.com/pod-product-compliance
Lightning Source LLC
Chambersburg PA
CBHW071313250626
47159CB00004B/1401